MW01125160

Books by Kathleen Suzette:

A Home Economics Mystery Series

Appliqued to Death
A Home Economics Mystery, book 1
Buttoned Up
A Home Economics Mystery, book 2

A Rainey Daye Cozy Mystery Series

Clam Chowder and a Murder
A Rainey Daye Cozy Mystery, book 1
A Short Stack and a Murder
A Rainey Daye Cozy Mystery, book 2
Cherry Pie and a Murder
A Rainey Daye Cozy Mystery, book 3
Barbecue and a Murder
A Rainey Daye Cozy Mystery, book 4
Birthday Cake and a Murder
A Rainey Daye Cozy Mystery, book 5
Hot Cider and a Murder
A Rainey Daye Cozy Mystery, book 6
Roast Turkey and a Murder
A Rainey Daye Cozy Mystery, book 7
Gingerbread and a Murder
A Rainey Daye Cozy Mystery, book 8
Fish Fry and a Murder
A Rainey Daye Cozy Mystery, book 9
Cupcakes and a Murder
A Rainey Daye Cozy Mystery, book 10

A Pumpkin Hollow Mystery Series

Candy Coated Murder

A Pumpkin Hollow Mystery, book 1
Murderously Sweet
A Pumpkin Hollow Mystery, book 2
Chocolate Covered Murder
A Pumpkin Hollow Mystery, book 3
Death and Sweets
A Pumpkin Hollow Mystery, book 4
Sugared Demise
A Pumpkin Hollow Mystery, book 5
Confectionately Dead
A Pumpkin Hollow Mystery, book 6
Hard Candy and a Killer
A Pumpkin Hollow Mystery, book 7
Candy Kisses and a Killer
A Pumpkin Hollow Mystery, book 8

A Freshly Baked Cozy Mystery Series
Apple Pie A La Murder,
A Freshly Baked Cozy Mystery, Book 1
Trick or Treat and Murder,
A Freshly Baked Cozy Mystery, Book 2
Thankfully Dead
A Freshly Baked Cozy Mystery, Book 3
Candy Cane Killer
A Freshly Baked Cozy Mystery, Book 4
Ice Cold Murder
A Freshly Baked Cozy Mystery, Book 5
Love is Murder
A Freshly Baked Cozy Mystery, Book 6
Strawberry Surprise Killer

A Freshly Baked Cozy Mystery, Book 7
A Gracie Williams Mystery Series
Pushing Up Daisies in Arizona,
A Gracie Williams Mystery, Book 1
Kicked the Bucket in Arizona,
A Gracie Williams Mystery, Book 2

Hard Candy and a Killer
A Pumpkin Hollow Mystery
By
Kathleen Suzette

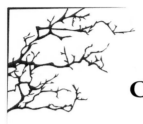

Chapter One

"MOM'S KILLING ME WITH all this fudge," Christy moaned.

I turned and looked at my sister. We were in the kitchen of our parents' shop, the Pumpkin Hollow Candy Store, packing up candy orders to be shipped out first thing in the morning. We had been selling candy online since last November, and business had been booming, particularly during the Christmas season. My dad had an outside job, selling insurance, but Mom had always worked the candy store, even before her parents handed it down to her years ago.

"How is she killing you?" I asked my sister, humoring her.

"She keeps coming up with these wonderful new fudge flavors, and I keep eating it. I told her she needed to cut that out, but she won't listen to me. You know how she is," she said with a laugh as she closed the small shipping box she had just packed with an order of peanut butter fudge.

I chuckled. "Well, you knew what you were getting yourself into when you came to work at a candy store." Christy had moved away from Pumpkin Hollow last fall, but when her marriage began to deteriorate, she moved back home in December and went to work with us at the candy store. We needed help with the increased orders we got from online customers.

"Sure, now you're going to bring logic into it. I need somebody to blame for my recent weight gain, and you're making it hard for me to dodge that responsibility."

"Yeah, well, sorry for making things harder for you," I said and finished wrapping two pounds of vanilla fudge for the next order. "Besides, it's not like she makes you pay for the fudge. It's a bonus for working here."

She eyed me. "I don't need that kind of bonus. I've got to lose ten pounds before summer, and you know how hard it is for me to lose weight. I think I must have gotten the weight gain genes in this family."

I looked her up and down. If my sister needed to lose ten pounds, then I needed to lose fifteen. "What are you talking about? You don't need to lose ten pounds."

"Yes, I do. I am footloose and fancy-free, and I am making some changes in my life. It's a new beginning for me."

I rolled my eyes at her. "Christy, you're fine the way you are. Seriously, don't let anyone tell you otherwise."

She shook her head. "Honestly, Mia, I've been thinking about it for the last few weeks, and I'm ready to move on. I think the divorce is a good idea."

"Maybe you should take things a little slower," I suggested as I wrapped a pound of chocolate fudge. "You haven't been separated from John for very long."

"I know, but I'm ready to move on. It's time."

"How are we doing on the orders, girls?" Mom asked, returning to the kitchen. "I feel like all I ever do is make fudge these days."

"That's because that's just about all you're doing," I told her. "We've got most of the orders ready to be shipped in the morning."

"Good, I'm glad to hear it," Mom said and went to the small desk in the corner of the kitchen. She peered at the computer screen, looking over the order queue. "Well, I guess I spoke too soon. We've got three more orders since I went out front."

I sighed. "The more orders the better, but business has really been picking up. We really need to hire more help."

"I told your father the same thing last night," she agreed without looking up from the computer screen.

In Pumpkin Hollow, we celebrated Halloween all year long. The official Halloween season ran from Labor Day weekend until a couple of weeks into November, but in the Halloween business district, the stores remain decorated for Halloween throughout the year. We were a popular tourist destination, and I was still surprised by the fact that we sold a fair amount of Halloween candy, even in the spring.

"I better get those bonbons out to the display case," Mom said, looking at the tray of candy on the counter.

"I'll take them for you," I offered and went to look over her shoulder at the orders in the order queue on the computer before I went. "Don't we have enough peanut butter fudge already made to ship for these orders?"

"I think we do," Mom said with a sigh. "I don't know what's gotten into me lately, I just feel tired all the time." She sighed again and then chuckled. "Listen to me. I've got too much work to do to be tired."

I looked at her. "Maybe you should make an appointment with the doctor?"

Recently Mom had been making comments about not feeling well and being tired all the time. I had chalked it up to the busy Christmas season and Valentine's Day, but things had slowed down considerably now that it was the middle of March, and I wondered why she was still so tired.

"I may need to do that," she said absently.

I picked up the tray of bonbons and headed out to the candy store floor. Our part-time help, Carrie Green, was filling shelves with packaged candy. My mother made most of the candy that we sold at the candy store, but we also had prepackaged candy that we shipped in and sold. I went to the display case, opened the back of it, and placed the tray of bonbons inside.

"What do you have planned for the weekend, Mia?" Carrie asked me.

"I don't know yet," I said. "Ethan has the weekend off, and I can hardly wait. We might just hang out at home and watch TV. I don't know, sometimes I think we're getting lazy in our relationship. We haven't been dating nearly long enough for that to happen."

She chuckled. "You two need to get out more. With spring here, there's a lot more to do," Carrie said. "Darryl and I are taking the girls to South Lake Tahoe for a kids' extravaganza. It's being put on by some of the businesses there and It'll keep them busy and happy for a few hours."

"That'll be fun. I bet they'll love it." Carrie had twin girls that had just turned three. They were a handful and kept Carrie and Darryl running all the time.

The bell over the door jingled, and we both looked up. Dr. Amy Jones, one of the local doctors, walked through the door. She stopped and smiled. "Hello ladies," she said brightly. "I'm supposed to be getting back to the office, but as I was driving by, it's almost as if the candy was calling my name." She laughed.

"I don't doubt it for a minute," I said. "My mother's candy has a way of doing that." I liked Dr. Jones. She was petite, with dark brown hair, and an infectious laugh.

"You can say that again," she agreed. She walked over to the display case and peered in. "I've had your mother's vanilla fudge on my mind for the past couple of weeks. I bought some before Christmas, and it didn't last long in my house. My husband loves it, too."

"The vanilla fudge is one of my favorites," I said. "Would you like some?"

"I would, but don't tell my husband. I told him I was staying away from sugar for a while after all I had eaten at Christmas time. But Christmas has been a while ago, so why don't you get me a half-pound, and I'll try to make it last."

I went to the display case and opened the back of it, pulling out the tray of vanilla fudge. "If you can make it last for very long, you've got more self-control than I do. I try not to bring any of it home because I know what's going to happen if I do."

She chuckled. "I won't bring it home, otherwise my husband will eat it all. I'm going to be greedy and keep it at the office for myself."

Mom came out from the back with a tray of hard candy pumpkins, goblins, and ghosts she had made using candy molds. "Hello, Dr. Jones," she said when she saw the doctor.

Dr. Jones smiled. "Hello Ann," she said. "I was just telling Mia that I couldn't resist your vanilla fudge. Honestly, vanilla-flavored anything is my favorite."

"Well, if you love vanilla, let me give you a couple of the vanilla ghosts I made," she said, walking up to the counter. She had individually wrapped each piece of the hard candy she carried on the tray, and she picked up two of the vanilla ghosts and gave them to the doctor. "No charge. I've been experimenting with flavorings, trying to get them more distinct without increasing the sweetness, and I really like how the vanilla turned out in these candies."

"Oh, that's sweet of you. Thanks, Ann," she said, taking the candies from my mother. "I will definitely not be sharing these with my husband. Don't tell him."

"I won't. I promise," Mom said, setting the tray on the front counter. "I've got to get in to see you soon. I've just been so tired lately, and it's time for a checkup, anyway."

"A lot of people have been complaining about feeling run down lately. Seems the winter doldrums are harder to shake off this year for some reason."

"You're probably right," Mom said. "That's probably all it is. I just need a couple of days off to rest and relax."

"I keep telling my husband I need a vacation," Dr. Jones said. "Just one week. Someplace to relax where it's nice and warm. But all he does is complain about having to leave the house for that length of time. That one is a homebody."

"My husband is the same way," Mom said. "Maybe we should just run off without our husbands and enjoy ourselves at the beach."

"That's a great idea," she agreed. "I just might take you up on that offer sometime soon."

I weighed out the vanilla fudge and wrapped it up for Dr. Jones, then put it in a bag with the two vanilla ghosts Mom had given her. I rang up her fudge and waited as she and Mom chatted another couple of minutes.

"Thanks, Mia," she finally said, removing her debit card from her purse. "Remember now, mums the word that I'm buying candy."

"Your secret is safe with me," I said. "No one will know about your vanilla addiction. I've got one of my own, and that kind of secret needs to be kept under wraps."

She laughed and ran her card through the card reader. When she left, I turned to Mom, and that was when I noticed how tired she really did look. I hoped it was just fatigue left over from the holidays and the cold weather, but the dark circles under her eyes made me wonder.

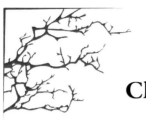

Chapter Two

I STOOD ON MY FRONT porch step and watched my boyfriend, Ethan Banks, pull into his driveway. Ethan was a police officer who did double duty as a detective when needed. I had moved in across the street from him last fall, and it had been a fun move for both of us. On his side of the street were six tiny white cottages with black shutters, and on my side of the street were a matching set of six more tiny white cottages with black shutters. My cat, Boo, intertwined himself between my legs as I waited for Ethan. Boo had been a stray that adopted me when I moved in. He was all black and completely cute.

When Ethan got out of his truck, he turned and waved to me. "How are you this evening, my love?" he called with a chuckle.

"I'm doing fantastic," I said. "If you're hungry, I made some spaghetti."

It was Sunday evening, and we hadn't gotten to spend nearly enough time together over the weekend as I had hoped. Ethan had been called into work when three other officers called in sick with the flu, and I ended up working Saturday afternoon at the candy store.

He grinned and trotted across the street. "You don't have to ask me twice," he said. When he got to me, he gave me a quick kiss, and we looked into each other's eyes for a moment. Then he gave me a longer, slower kiss. He pulled back and looked at me again. "I feel like I have the better end of this deal. You're always making dinner for me."

"I have to eat, anyway. It's not like it's hard making enough food for two," I said with a shrug. "Besides that, I get home before you do, so I may as well make dinner for us."

"We'll have to go out to dinner next weekend then. I'll take you someplace nice. You choose the restaurant."

"That sounds like fun," I said, and we turned and headed into my house.

He stopped and scooped up Boo on his way in, rubbing his ears. "Boo, how are you doing today? Did you catch any mice or birds?"

Boo responded by purring and rubbing his head against his chest.

"I think that means he's doing pretty darn well," I said with a chuckle as I headed to the kitchen. "I've told him he isn't allowed to catch any critters. I don't want him bringing them into the house."

"I guess there are some drawbacks to his hunting." He looked at me, one eyebrow raised. "You didn't happen to think about making garlic bread, did you?"

"Of course I did," I said. "What's spaghetti without the garlic bread?"

"You can say that again," he agreed as I went to the stove to check on the pasta.

"So, how are things going at work?" I asked as I stirred the pasta so it wouldn't stick together.

"Pretty good if you want to know the truth," he said. "No one's killed anyone in months, and the biggest case I have to work on is a robbery at the lumberyard."

I looked at him, eyebrows raised. "Someone robbed the lumberyard?"

"Yeah, they cut a hole in the chain-link fence at the back of the yard where the lumber is stored and made off with some wood. We got a blurry picture on security cameras, but it's going to be tough to make an ID from that."

"Why can't people just leave things alone if it doesn't belong to them?" It annoyed me that it didn't seem to bother some people to steal.

"Easy now," he said with a chuckle. "If all the criminals disappeared, what would I do for a job?"

"You could work with me at my mother's candy shop," I suggested. I turned the fire off on the burner beneath the pot of pasta, grabbed two potholders, and took the pot to the sink to drain.

"I hadn't thought of that. That's not a bad idea. A candy shop job comes with fringe benefits. I can eat all the candy I want," he said, grinning. "I'm tempted."

"Well, maybe not all you want. We don't want to put Mom out of business." I leaned back as I poured the water out of the pot, and steam billowed up.

"Then I better stick with police work. If I can't eat all the candy I want, I'll have to pass." He put Boo down on the floor. "Can I help you with something?"

"There's some iced tea in the refrigerator if you want to get it and pour us some," I said.

"You got it." He got the pitcher of iced tea from the fridge and some glasses from the cupboard. "I appreciate you making dinner."

"I enjoy doing it. The garlic bread is done, and we're ready to eat," I said. I poured the spaghetti sauce over the pasta and set the bowl on the table, then took the garlic bread out of the oven. It was a simple meal, which is my favorite kind. It was just fun to be able to spend some time together in the evenings after work.

"Tomorrow night I'll stop off and pick up something for dinner," Ethan promised as he washed up, and we sat down at the table.

"I've been thinking about new ideas to bring more tourists to town during the off-season," I said as he put some spaghetti onto his plate. "I mentioned a while back that I thought we should have a mini-Halloween season during the summer, and the more I think about it, the more I think that's what we should do. If we get some advertising going, I think we could see a nice uptick in business during the summer."

He nodded. "I think it's a great idea. Maybe we could draw more tourists in."

I nodded and cut the garlic bread. "I think so. I'm not sure what the dates should be, though. We want to give everyone a break before the official Halloween season begins on Labor Day weekend."

"How about July? People are on vacation, and they need someplace to go, so why not come to Pumpkin Hollow?" he suggested.

I twirled some spaghetti onto my fork. "That's what I was thinking. Maybe have it run for two weeks in July. That gives us about six weeks to recover before the Halloween season, and hopefully, it will keep the tourists from getting burned out."

"You might be overthinking that," he said. "I think people really enjoy coming to Pumpkin Hollow, and it wouldn't surprise me a bit if the same people who come during the fall come during the summer as well."

"You may be right about that," I agreed and took a bite of my spaghetti. "I love the idea of a mini-Halloween season during the summer. I was thinking we might call it Pumpkin Hollow Days to differentiate the events. That way people wouldn't think they'd be coming to see the same old thing. We would have to come up with some ideas for events, and with the input of the other business owners and townsfolk, I think we can put on something fun for the summer."

"We'll come up with new ideas," Ethan said. "As soon as you get the dates figured out, let me know, and I'll plan my vacation at a different time. Maybe the two of us can go on vacation somewhere when Pumpkin Hollow Days has ended."

"That would be fun," I said. "What do you have in mind?"

He shrugged. "To be honest, I don't have anything in mind just yet, but we'll figure something out. Maybe we can go to the beach."

I nodded. Ethan and I had only been dating for a few months, but there had been something comfortable about our relationship from the very beginning. Taking a vacation together would be fun.

When we finished dinner, we watched television and discussed what we could do during Pumpkin Hollow Days.

IT WAS THE MIDDLE OF the night, and I was sleeping soundly when Boo jumped on my back and meowed loudly.

"What do you want, Boo?" I mumbled. "There's food in your bowl. Go eat it and leave me alone."

Boo started kneading my back, and I groaned as his nails poked through my pajamas and into my back. "Boo, I need some sleep. I've got to get up in the morning and go to work."

Boo purred loudly and meowed again. That was when I opened my eyes. There was an orange glow outside my bedroom window. I rolled to the side to let Boo off my back and onto the bed and I hurried to my feet, sliding my feet into my slippers. I went to the window and pulled back the curtain. A house on the next block was on fire.

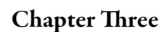

Chapter Three

I RAN TO MY CLOSET and quickly got dressed. Sirens blared in the distance, and I hurriedly pulled my boots on and grabbed my cell phone. It was 2:03 a.m. The shock of seeing the fire had cleared my head for a moment, but now I felt woozy from the lack of sleep after staying up later than I normally did.

Boo meowed and rubbed against my legs. "I'll be back in a few minutes, Boo," I said and ran my hand over his head. Hurrying to the front door, I grabbed my coat and house keys from the hook near the front door. The freezing night air hit me as I stepped outside. Lights in the neighboring houses came on as the fire trucks pulled up to the house with their sirens blaring.

I headed across the street as Ethan walked out his front door. He looked at me and then looked at the house that was on fire. The house was on the corner on the next block and had been vacant for a few weeks. A 'for rent' sign was in the front window. It was an older, large two-story home, and until recently, had been rented for as long as I had lived in my little cottage.

There was melting snow in the street, and I picked my way carefully through it, trying not to slip on the road surface. "Wow," I said to Ethan when I got to him. "That's a big fire."

He nodded, taking hold of my hand. "Hopefully they'll be able to save the house."

"I wonder who called the fire department?"

"I called them as soon as I woke up, but someone else had already called it in."

We could feel the heat from the fire as we stood and watched the firemen go to work, pulling hoses from the trucks. The sky was black with a new moon, and the fire cast an eery glow on the neighborhood.

"I'm glad somebody was awake to call the fire department," I said, moving closer to Ethan.

"You can say that again. It wouldn't take much for the house next door to catch fire," Ethan agreed. We watched as the firemen worked on the fire, and more neighbors came out of their houses. Two more firetrucks showed up and helped battle the blaze, along with three police cars and an ambulance.

I glanced at Ethan. "Did someone move into that house yet?" I asked. As far as I knew, the house was still vacant, and I hoped there wasn't a need for the ambulance.

"No, I don't think so. I'm sure they called for the ambulance just in case."

I breathed a sigh of relief, glad the house was still empty, but it made me wonder how the fire had started. As we watched, I was amazed at how quickly the fire began to come down. Ethan and I walked to the corner where one of the police officers had parked.

"Hey, Justin," Ethan said to the officer. "What do you know about the fire?"

He shrugged. "I don't know much of anything yet," he said. "An emergency call came in that the house was on fire, and that's about it."

"It should be vacant," Ethan informed him. "The renters moved out a few weeks ago, and there's been a 'for rent' sign in the front window since then."

He nodded. "Good to know. Could be some vagrants broke in and started it, or maybe it was an electrical fire due to faulty wiring."

We watched as the firefighters worked on bringing the flames down, and two more of our neighbors came out of their houses to stand with us.

"They're getting that knocked down fast," our neighbor, Billy Carnes, said. "I'd hate to see that thing spread to nearby houses or for the second story to cave in."

"That would be terrible," I said as we watched the flames come down. "I'm glad it was spotted in time."

He nodded. "I saw some homeless people hanging out around there last week. I called the police, and they made them leave, but maybe they came back. Wouldn't surprise me if they got in there and started a fire to keep warm, and it got away from them."

Ethan glanced at him. "Do you remember what they looked like?"

He shrugged. "It was a man and a woman pushing a shopping cart. They were maybe in their thirties. I didn't talk to them, so I didn't see them up close."

This was news to me. I hadn't realized Pumpkin Hollow had a homeless population. "Do we have a lot of homeless people here?" I asked, looking at Ethan.

"We've got a small handful of homeless folk wandering around town. Mostly they keep to themselves and don't cause any trouble." He eyed the burning house thoughtfully.

I wrapped my arms around myself and shivered. I couldn't imagine being homeless during the winter where it snowed as it did here. How did they stay warm? And why hadn't I noticed them? "Do they all push shopping carts? It seems like I would have noticed them."

"No, I've never seen any of them pushing shopping carts. They usually just carry most of their things in bags or backpacks. We occasionally get a call from one of the merchants with complaints about them loitering around their stores, and we ask them what they're doing there. Most of the time they don't have any place else to go."

That made me sad. I wondered if they had family here in town, or if they were just passing through. I thought I knew most of the people that lived in Pumpkin Hollow, but maybe these people weren't local.

"I hope they weren't in there when the fire started," I said. I suddenly felt sick to my stomach. If they had built a fire to keep warm and had gone to sleep, they may not have woken up and gotten out of the house in time.

"Me too," Ethan said. "Maybe it was just an electrical fire."

I hoped that's what it was. I also hoped the owner of the house had their insurance policy up to date on it.

It only took about thirty minutes to put the fire out. The neighbors that had come out of their houses slowly wandered back home and went back to bed. But Ethan and I waited and watched, leaning against the police officer's car.

"You should go back to bed," Ethan finally said to me. "You've got to get to work in the morning."

"You have to work in the morning, too," I pointed out. Although it was cold outside, I hesitated to go back to bed just yet. I was fully awake now, and I didn't know if I could go back to sleep, anyway.

"Yes I do, smarty-pants," Ethan said and wrapped his arm around my shoulders. "We both should go back to bed. We aren't doing anything helpful just standing out here watching."

I sighed. "Now that I'm wide awake, I doubt I'll be able to go back to sleep. I think the fire scared Boo, and that was why he woke me up."

He smiled. "Boo is a good watch-cat. He'll let you know when trouble starts."

"He's earning his cat treats that way," I said with a chuckle. "Everyone has to earn their keep at my house, you know."

"Good to know," he said.

We watched as one of the firemen said something to another fireman, and he followed him back inside the house. There was suddenly a flurry of activity at the front door as some of the firemen went inside the house.

"Wonder what's going on?" I asked.

"I don't know, but I'm going to go find out," he said and headed across the street.

I didn't know if he wanted me to come with him, but I followed along behind him. One of the officers was standing near the door, and when he saw Ethan, he came over to him.

"What's going on?" Ethan asked him.

The officer glanced at me and then turned back to Ethan. "There's a body inside the house."

My stomach dropped.

Chapter Four

"I'M BEAT," CHRISTY said. "When I get off work, I'm going to crash. I'm not used to getting here at 4:00 a.m."

"I don't blame you. I don't know how Mom does it every day," I said. "Was Mom not feeling well again?"

"She had a doctor's appointment," she said, looking across the kitchen at me. "I heard there was a fire on your street. What happened?"

I looked up from the hard candy pumpkins I was packing up to ship out for an Internet order. "Boo woke me up in the middle of the night, and I saw an orange glow outside my window. When I looked out, I saw the house on the corner of the next block on fire. Ethan and I went outside to watch the firefighters put it out, but I haven't heard anything from him since early this morning."

"That's scary," she said as she affixed a shipping label to the box she had just packed. "I'm glad it didn't spread to other houses."

"I'll say," I agreed. "They found a body." I said the last part quietly so no one out front could hear me.

She turned to look at me in surprise. "A body? Inside the burning house?"

I nodded. "Yes, the house has been vacant for several weeks, but the firefighters found a body inside. One of my neighbors said they had seen homeless people hanging around, so it may have been one of them."

"Wow," she said as she took the box to the shelf where we put the finished orders until the mail person picked them up. "How awful. I wonder if they started the fire to stay warm, or if there was foul play involved."

"I'm wondering the same thing," I said and put the gift box with the pumpkins inside a shipping box.

Mom came into the kitchen. "Good morning, girls. It's a lovely, sunny day today. What's going on with you two?"

I was glad to see Mom looking a little more chipper than she had lately. "Not a lot. We were just talking about the house that caught fire in my neighborhood last night."

She stopped and looked at me. "I hadn't heard about that," she said. "Did it burn down completely?"

"No, not completely, but they found a body in it. The house has been vacant for a few weeks, and there's some suspicion that it might be a homeless person that was trying to stay warm."

She shook her head, making a clucking sound in her throat. "I hate to hear that."

"I guess that means Ethan's on another case then," Christy added.

"I suppose so," I said. "If it looks like it was an accident, I think it should be a pretty quick case."

"I hope it was an accident," Mom said and went to the sink to wash her hands.

"Christy said you went to the doctor this morning, Mom," I said as Christy sealed the shipping box. "And FYI, I'm glad you didn't ask me to come in because it was 3:30 in the morning by the time I got back to bed."

She chuckled. "Oh, Dr. Jones called me late Friday afternoon and told me she could squeeze me in for an appointment first thing this morning. But when I got there, the nurse said she hadn't come into work yet." She shrugged. "He said she didn't call him and let him know she wouldn't be there, and he didn't know when she would be in. I told him it was fine, and I'd call back and reschedule another appointment later in the week. At least I got to sleep in."

"That's odd that she didn't call her nurse to let him know she wouldn't be in," I said, picking up another order from the printer.

"Maybe she got sick in the night and overslept this morning," Mom said as she tied an apron around herself. "Now then, I need to get some candy making done. Christy, what needs to be made this morning?"

"We probably need more chocolate fudge without nuts, vanilla fudge, and more of that cherry chip fudge. I have a couple of Internet orders, and I noticed the cherry chip fudge tray out front was getting low."

She nodded. "I'll get right on it."

When I finished packing the orders we had completed, I went back out front to see how things were going. With it being spring, the walk-in customers weren't as plentiful as they were at other times of the year. Our part-time help, Carrie Green, was finishing waiting on a customer, and she turned and grinned at me. "We've had more customers than usual this morning."

"Have we? I've been packing orders, so I hadn't noticed," I said, glancing at the wrought iron clock over the door. It was 10:30, and Carrie had been here since 6:30. "Carrie, why don't you go ahead and go home? Things will be slow until later this afternoon. I can cover it."

"Are you sure? I can hang out longer if you need me to," she said, turning to me.

"It will be fine," I said as I went to the display case and removed an empty tray. "You go home and give those little cuties of yours a squeeze for me."

"I'll see you tomorrow then," she said and removed her apron. "I've got tons of errands to run today, anyway. Have a good day."

"You too," I said.

I went around the store making sure everything was neat and tidy, and the shelves were filled. Mom had gotten some new prepackaged candy-coated cookies in, and I took a look at them. I could smell the vanilla through the cellophane wrapping. They were shaped like spring flowers and butterflies with pastel-colored candy coating.

The bell over the front door jingled, and I looked up as Ethan walked in. He smiled tiredly at me. "Hey."

"Hey yourself," I said and went to him. "You look tired." I put my arms around him, and he gave me a quick kiss.

He chuckled. "Thanks, that's how I want my girlfriend to greet me every day—you look terrible."

I playfully slapped at his arm. "I did not say you look terrible. I said you looked tired, and you *should* be tired. What time did you get to bed?"

"I haven't," he said, sighing.

"I guess that explains why you look tired then," I said. "Let me get you some fudge. That'll help wake you up, at least for a few minutes. Until the sugar crash happens, but you'll enjoy the high while it lasts." I went back behind the front counter. "What would you like?"

He shrugged. "I don't know if it really matters if you want to know the truth. I'm just beat."

I looked at him. "Ethan Banks is turning down fudge? Are you sick?"

"Hold on now. I didn't say I was turning it down," he said, leaning on the front counter. "I'm just too tired to care about what kind. You pick."

I nodded and cut him a piece of the cherry chip fudge. It was one of his favorites, and I thought he would change his mind about not caring what kind of fudge I gave him when he had it in his hands. I put the fudge on a piece of waxed paper and slid it across the counter to him. "This should brighten your day."

"Oh, you're not playing fair now," he said and picked it up and took a bite. He groaned. "Your mom makes the best fudge. Thanks. I needed this."

"You need some caffeine, too," I said, closing the display case door.

"I've had three cups of coffee this morning. Large cups. I'll probably have three more before the morning is over."

"Any idea who the body was in the house?" I asked, leaning on the front counter.

He looked at me, eyebrows raised. "Maybe. This is between the two of us, but Dr. Jones' husband reported her missing Saturday morning."

I gasped. "She was in here Friday morning. My mom had an appointment with her this morning, and her nurse said she didn't show up. Does her husband have any idea what might have happened to her?"

"No, she worked late at the office Friday night, and she never came home. Around eight o'clock that evening, he went to the office to look for her, but the office was locked up. I haven't had a chance to talk to him yet. I'm just going off of the missing person's report, but I'm heading over to talk to him now."

The possibility of the dead body being Dr. Amy Jones made me sick. I couldn't imagine what she might have been doing in that house. "I hope it's not her. I hope there was just some sort of miscommunication between her and her husband, and she'll be home any time now." I knew that was a stretch, but I was hoping for the best.

He nodded and took another bite of the fudge. "This is really good. I think I'm going to stop by the bakery and get some coffee before I head over to talk to Mr. Jones. Without a fresh dose of caffeine, I might nod off, and I don't want him to think I don't care about his missing wife."

"That's probably a good idea," I agreed as he blinked and shook his head to stay awake. "I'm hoping that body they found in the house was someone else."

"You and me both," he said, picking up a napkin to take with him. "I better get going. I'm not going to get any sleep for a while, and if I don't keep moving, I'm going to be in trouble."

I nodded and gave him a quick kiss before he left. "I'll see you tonight."

I couldn't imagine how Amy would end up dead in an empty house. If it was her, I was sure foul play was involved, and that was the last thing I would have expected to happen to her. She was a favorite doctor in town.

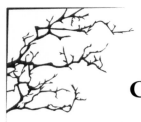

Chapter Five

THAT EVENING AFTER I'd gotten off work, I picked up dinner to take to Amy's husband, Steve Jones. Amy and Steve were in their mid-thirties and had grown up in Pumpkin Hollow. They had gone off to college after high school with Amy going to med school in Los Angeles and then moved back so Amy could start her practice here. My family had known them for as long as I could remember.

There was a mom and pop restaurant in town that specialized in chicken, both roasted and fried, along with all the sides. I had run into Steve picking up dinner there several times, and I was sure he would welcome the meal. With the stress of his wife missing, I thought he probably hadn't had time to think about cooking or eating a proper meal. If he wasn't hungry, he could always put it in the refrigerator and eat it later.

When Steve came to the door, he looked surprised to see me. "Mia."

"Hi Steve," I said. "I heard Amy was missing. I'm so sorry to hear it. I thought I'd pick up dinner for you and let you know that my thoughts and prayers are with you both. My parents and sister send their love."

His eyes teared up. "That's kind of you, Mia. Would you like to come in?"

I nodded and followed him into the house. The Joneses lived in a conservative part of town with newer, recently built homes. The inside of their house was decorated farmhouse style, and it was cozy with its light colors and wood finishes.

"Please, have a seat, Mia," he said as I handed him the bag with the chicken dinner in it. I had bought the whole chicken with sides so he would have leftovers for the next several days. "That was kind of you to think about me. Let me put this in the kitchen, and I'll be right back."

I sat down and looked around the room. The Joneses didn't have any children, and I recalled Amy saying they were waiting until her medical practice was better established until they had them. But she had been in practice for almost ten years, so I wasn't sure why they hadn't had any yet.

Steve returned to the living room. "That's sweet of you to think of me, Mia. Thank you," he said. He took a seat on the sofa across from me. "I've hardly eaten a thing since Amy didn't come home Friday evening. The stress of it all is more than I can stand."

"I can't imagine how hard this must be. Do you have any idea where she may have gone?" I asked. I hoped he didn't take offense to the question, but I had to wonder if he at least had some idea what had happened to her. Maybe she had planned to run an errand after work, and something happened along the way.

He shook his head, his hands clasped together in his lap. "Sometimes she stays late at the office, especially on Friday nights, so she can get caught up on paperwork. I didn't think anything of it when she didn't make it home by six o'clock. When it was eight o'clock, and she hadn't answered her phone or called me back, I went down to the office to take see if she was still working and lost track of time. It was dark and closed up." He shook his head. "I don't know what could have happened to her. It doesn't make sense, and I've been worried sick ever since."

The anguish in his voice nearly brought me to tears. "I'm so sorry," I said. "I know the police are doing everything they can to find her."

What do you say to someone whose wife had just disappeared? I didn't want to bring up the body in the house that had caught fire, but I was sure he knew about it. Ethan would have asked him questions regarding his missing wife, and I felt sure he would have mentioned the body.

"I spoke with Ethan Banks this morning," he said, his eyes going to something just past my shoulder for a moment. Then he made eye contact again. "There was a body found in a house that caught fire last night."

"I know, I live over on the next block from it," I said. I hated that there was a possibility that it was Amy.

He nodded, his hands intertwining with one another. "I can't imagine how it could be her. But he wouldn't ask me the questions he did unless he thought there was a possibility it was Amy, right? It was in this morning's newspaper, too. The fact that a body was found in that house. But I don't see how it can be her. What would she be doing in a vacant house?" He looked at me, pleading with his eyes for me to give him some reason that it couldn't be her.

I shook my head slowly. "At this point, I doubt the police have any solid information on who it was they found in that house. One of my neighbors mentioned he had seen homeless people around, so it could have been one of them." I didn't want him to give up hope that Amy might be found alive. I couldn't imagine my spouse not coming home from work one day and not being able to get ahold of him.

"I know," he said, nodding. "That's what Ethan said. He said someone had mentioned homeless people hanging around the house. But that still leaves me with the puzzle as to what happened to Amy. She wouldn't just up and leave me, you know." His voice cracked when he said it.

"Of course not," I said, shaking my head. "I know Amy, and she's not the sort of person that would just run off without telling you where she was going. Besides that, she's got a medical practice—people depend on her. She would never just leave like that." As soon as I said it, I felt badly. Because if she hadn't left of her own choice, that meant she had left by force.

He stared at me, quiet a moment. "I refuse to think that that body might be her."

I nodded. "I refuse to believe it, too," I said, reassuring him. I didn't know what else to say about it. He needed some hope that she would be found alive somewhere. And then he would have to deal with the reason she had left. But for now, we would concentrate on her not being dead. There was no kind way to put it. Either Amy abandoned him, or someone forced her to leave.

"I'll tell you something," he said, running a finger under his chin. "If something did happen to Amy, if that is her body in that house, I know exactly who did it."

This took me by surprise. "Who do you think would do it?"

"Her nurse, Rick Newsom. I never trusted that guy. He looks like a model and a bodybuilder, and yet he's a nurse. Why would someone become a nurse when they look like that? Who does that?"

What he said surprised me. What difference did it make if Rick Newsom looked like a bodybuilder? If he enjoyed nursing, then that was all that mattered. "A lot of men are nurses these days. I guess he felt it was what would make him happy." I didn't know what else to say.

He shook his head. "That's not what I meant. I mean, look at him. He looks like a movie star. Why would he waste his life as a nurse?"

I still wasn't sure what he was getting at. "The nursing profession is an honorable profession. I can see why a lot of people would choose it, man or woman," I said slowly. "Why do you think he might have hurt Amy?"

"He complains that she doesn't pay him enough. He thinks he's worth a lot more money. But he doesn't take into consideration that this is Pumpkin Hollow, a small town. You don't get the same kind of money here that you would in a larger city. And he always complains about everything Amy asks him to do."

"So he's unhappy working for Amy?" I asked, taking this in.

He nodded. "He hates working for Amy. Amy has overheard him complaining to the other staff. His attitude is terrible. He's always angry about something. Amy has gotten to where she's afraid to ask him to do anything."

I didn't think the fact that he was unhappy at his job was reason enough to kill his boss. "Did he ever threaten Amy?"

"He wouldn't come right out and say what he wanted to do," he said, rubbing his hands on his knees. "But, one day he told Amy he wasn't going to be treated the way she was treating him. He said one day she would be sorry for it."

I was surprised. I couldn't imagine Amy treating anyone unkindly. "What kind of treatment was he referring to?"

He sighed and sat back on the sofa. "He said she was disrespectful to him. That she embarrassed him in front of patients."

That didn't sound like Amy. "What did Amy say when he said she would be sorry?"

"She tried to get him to explain exactly what she had done to upset him. I told her she needed to fire him, but you know how she is. She doesn't want to hurt anyone's feelings, and she refused to do it."

"Did you tell all of this to Ethan?"

He nodded. "I did. I don't know if Ethan thought what I told him was compelling or not," he said. "But there's just something about this guy. When I go into the office to visit Amy, he always has a sneer on his face. Like he thinks he's better than everyone else."

"Ethan will speak to him," I assured him. It didn't seem like what Steve was saying about Rick was enough motive for murder. There had to be something else going on for Steve to think he might kill Amy. "Was there anything else that happened between them?"

He nodded. "He has a good reason to get even with her. His grandmother was a patient of Amy's. She died from complications of pneumonia. He said he told Amy she needed to admit his grandmother to the hospital. Amy decided the illness wasn't severe enough, and she wrote her a prescription for antibiotics and told her to come back to the office in the morning if she wasn't any better. But she died in the middle of the night. Rick was furious and screamed at Amy—threatening to sue her. She told him to take a week off from work. Doctors aren't perfect. There's only so much they can do for a patient. Sometimes people take a sudden turn for the worse, and that's what happened to his grandmother."

"Wow. I can see where he would be upset, but if she was elderly, her health may have been fragile to begin with," I said. I could also see where this would be a sticky situation for both Amy and Rick. "Why didn't Rick just take his grandmother to the hospital if he thought it was that serious?"

"That's what I asked, but Amy said he just kept blaming her."

I wasn't sure what to make of all of this, but if Rick's attitude was as bad as Steve was saying it was, and when you added that to his grandmother dying, there might be reason enough for him to take out his frustrations on Amy. When I went to see Amy as a patient, I didn't pick up on any animosity from Rick toward Amy. But I had only seen him at Amy's office twice, and those two visits might have been better days for both of them. It was worth checking into.

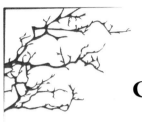

Chapter Six

"AH, COFFEE, BEAUTIFUL coffee," I said as Amanda handed me the mocha latte I had just ordered. My friend Amanda owns the Little Coffee Shop of Horrors, and I had been short of caffeine all week long. It was time to set things right.

"There's nothing like coffee in the morning, is there?" she asked with a chuckle.

"You can say that again," I said and took a deep swig of sweet goodness.

"Are you going to hang out for a few minutes? I'll have a coffee and sit with you if you are," she said.

I nodded. "I'm not due at the candy store for another half hour."

"Great," she said. "I'll get my coffee, and Trina can run the front counter for me."

When she made a coffee for herself, we headed over to a corner table and sat down. Amanda was my best friend from high school, and she was marrying Brian Shoate, a guy I had dated briefly in high school. They were going to be married in

June, and she had asked me to be the maid of honor and Christy to be a bridesmaid.

She leaned forward over the table. "So there was a fire on your block?"

I nodded. "Yes, the house on the corner on the next block."

"That's what I heard. I also heard they found a body in the house," she whispered. There were only three other customers in the coffee shop, and they were on the other side of the room. "I also heard it might be Dr. Jones."

I took another sip of my drink. I didn't know how much she knew, and I didn't want to tell her anything that I shouldn't. "She's a missing person at this point, and no one knows if that was her in the house or not. Honestly, there's a good chance it's a homeless person because the house has been vacant for a few weeks after the last renters moved out."

She sat back and nodded. "I hope it's not Dr. Jones. She's so sweet, and I just can't imagine how she could end up in a fire in an empty house."

"That's exactly my thinking. What would she have been in there for?" I took a sip of my coffee, my eyes going to the small centerpiece on each of the tables. There were small ceramic pumpkins in a circle of artificial spring flowers. "New centerpieces?"

She nodded. "It was time for a change. Ethan will have his hands full on this one, won't he?" she asked and took a drink of her coffee.

"He really will. I just hope Dr. Jones shows up soon. Of course, that's kind of a stretch, because why would she have just disappeared like that? I can't see her abandoning her marriage and her practice."

She nodded. "I don't think she would've left of her own choice, which makes me sad."

I hated talking about Amy this way. She was a sweet person, and I still really hoped there was some plausible explanation for why she had disappeared.

"How are the wedding plans going?" I asked, changing the subject. I took another sip of my drink and smiled. I didn't drink large quantities of coffee, but I did drink it every day, and I enjoyed it. I could feel the caffeine working the sleep right out of me.

"I need to call La Bella Bridal Shop and check on my dress. My mom is so excited, I don't know if she's going to be able to wait until June to see me get married."

I chuckled. "Your mom is so funny. She gets excited about everything. It's one of her best qualities."

She nodded and agreed. "I think so, too. I swear, she couldn't be negative about anything if she wanted to be. I'm probably feeling a little smug, but I think the wedding plans are going well. We've all ordered our dresses, and Brian and I have picked out the cake and the flower arrangements. Everything's going smoothly."

"I can hardly wait for the big day," I said. I was so happy she and Brian had finally set a date. They made a great couple, and I knew they'd be happy together.

"You know, most bridesmaids and maids of honor dread doing all the little things that are involved in helping a bride with the wedding," she said with a chuckle. "But you're going to be my cheerleader, aren't you?"

"Of course I am," I said. "I don't know about Christy, though. I think we're going to be doing well just to have her participate." My sister had been going through a tough time since separating from her husband. She had moped through the Christmas season. Not that I blamed her, because I'd feel the same way if it were me.

"How is she doing these days?" she asked.

"She actually seems to be doing better. She's made up her mind that she's going to go through with the divorce and not fight it. That makes me sad, but I understand."

"I never saw it coming. I always thought she and John were happy together."

"You and me both," I said. "Unfortunately, she thought they were happy, too."

We looked up as the door opened, and Christy walked through it. She waved at us and went up to the front counter to order a coffee. When she got her coffee, she came over and sat down at our table.

"You escaped the candy shop?" I asked her.

She nodded. "We had a lull, and I told Mom I needed some coffee. What are you girls talking about?"

I glanced at Amanda, and she looked back, wide-eyed. "The wedding," I said, feeling guilty about talking about her divorce.

"We're going to have to make an appointment soon to try on our dresses," Amanda said.

She nodded and took a sip of her coffee. "Well, today's a big day for me."

"Oh?" I asked.

She nodded again. "I filed for divorce." She looked at us, her eyes tearing up. She blinked them back and forced herself to smile.

I was shocked. I knew she was going to do it, but I thought that was something that would happen sometime in the next few months. "How did you manage to do that? You've been working at the candy store nearly every day."

"I filed online. Can you believe it?" she asked and laughed. "Won't John be shocked when he gets the papers?"

"You can file online? I had no idea," I said.

She nodded. "Yep. I can't think of anything more convenient. Just file the paperwork from the comfort of your own home. What could be simpler?"

"Well, Christy," Amanda said slowly. "I want to say I'm happy for you, but I'm really not. I mean, don't get me wrong, I am happy that you're doing what you feel like you need to do. But I can't be happy that you're getting a divorce."

"You did what you had to do," I said, squeezing Christy's hand.

"That's okay," she said, looking away. "You don't have to be happy for me. It's what John wanted, and I decided I'm not going to stand in his way."

"We're here for you," I promised.

She turned to me. "What does Ethan say about the body in the house that burned down?" she asked, changing the subject.

My sister didn't fool me. She might pretend that she was happy about the divorce, but I knew deep inside she still loved John, and this would be difficult for her to get through.

"It's still too early in the investigation to know much of anything yet."

"I heard there's a possibility it was Dr. Jones. Is that true? We just talked to her on Friday," Christy reminded me.

I sighed. "I hope not. Like I said, it's too early to know anything yet."

"Why didn't you tell me it might be her?" she asked and took a sip of her drink.

I shrugged. "They don't know for sure if it's her. I just didn't want to say anything until they identify the body."

"I hope it isn't true," Amanda said.

"I heard she and her husband weren't getting along well," Christy said. "But you didn't hear that from me."

"Who did you hear it from?" I asked her. I didn't know anything about Amy's marriage, let alone anything else about her personal life. I liked both her and her husband, and I thought they were happy.

"Fagan Branigan came into the candy shop and said he heard them arguing when he had a doctor's appointment a couple of months ago. Her husband had come into the office, and she took time away from seeing patients to talk to him."

I was shocked. "Seriously? He just came into her office and started arguing with her where everyone could hear them?"

"Fagan said he was trying to keep his voice down, but the walls are thin in that office, and he could tell Steve was angry."

"Did he hear anything specific?" I asked. It may have been nosy, asking about their argument, but I didn't care. Someone had to know where Amy was, and if it was her husband, he wasn't volunteering the information.

She shook her head. "No, he said he couldn't hear anything clearly, just that he could tell the tone of his voice was angry."

"A lot of married couples argue, and it doesn't mean anything," I pointed out. It did make me wonder, but at this point, there was no way to know what happened to Amy. I hoped things would turn out well, but the possibility of that happening was shrinking by the moment.

"I've always liked both Amy and her husband," Amanda said. "I think they make a cute couple, and like you said, everyone argues. It doesn't mean much of anything."

"That's true," Christy agreed. "I just hope they find her soon."

"We all hope that. Amanda, are you going to have your wedding reception at the ballroom?" I asked, changing the subject back to the wedding. I was beginning to feel depressed about the possibility that Amy was dead, and I didn't want to talk about it anymore.

She chuckled. "You would ask me that," she said. "Both Brian and I are hesitant, considering there were a couple of murders there. But if we don't have it there, I'm not sure where we'll have it." She sighed. "Maybe I'm not as on top of things as I thought I was. I need to get someplace booked, or we'll have to have my wedding here at the coffee shop."

I laughed. It didn't surprise me that Amanda and Brian were having second thoughts about having their wedding reception at the ballroom. After two people died there last December, I would have had second thoughts, too. And maybe even third and fourth thoughts.

"You'll get it worked out," I told her.

I sat back in my chair and took a long drink of my coffee, closing my eyes. At this point, I really just hoped we would be able to find Amy Jones alive and that she would be doing well, wherever she was. But I thought the chances of that were pretty slim.

Chapter Seven

IT WAS LATE IN THE afternoon when Ethan walked into the candy store. I looked up from helping a customer and smiled at him. When I was finished with the customer, and she left the shop, I turned to him.

"You look well-rested," I said as he leaned over and gave me a quick kiss.

He chuckled. "I don't know if I would say well-rested, but I certainly feel better than I did yesterday."

"Well, you certainly look better today," I said, walking over to one of the display shelves where I was unpacking some small stuffed owls and pumpkins. They were made of felt and would make cute shelf accents.

An eyebrow arched upwards as he watched me. "Are you trying to say that I didn't look good yesterday?"

I laughed. "No, I'm not trying to say you didn't look good yesterday. Stop it. You always look good. Have you found out anything new about the case?" I turned to look at him.

He looked around the empty candy store. "The body they found in the burned house was Amy Jones." His mouth formed a straight line.

I gasped, placing one hand on my chest. "Are you serious? Do you know that for sure?" I knew there was a good possibility it was her, but I hadn't wanted to believe it.

He nodded. "I wish I wasn't. We obtained dental records from her dentist, and it was an exact match."

"But doesn't that take time to process? I mean, how did the lab get the results so quickly?" I had expected identification of the body to take a while.

"Dental records are one of the quickest ways to identify a body. And of course, we knew where we were looking since we knew Amy was missing. The medical examiner got the x-rays yesterday and told us this morning." He shook his head. "I hated to hear it. I was hoping it wasn't her."

Sadness overwhelmed me. Amy was such a kind person that I couldn't imagine someone wanting to kill her. "I feel terrible about this."

"I feel bad about it, too," he said. "A lot of people really liked her in this town. It's a shame."

"Well, *someone* didn't like her," I said thoughtfully. "I wonder what she was doing in that house? An empty house is a weird place for her to be."

"That's the question of the day. But we'll figure it out."

"Are you done investigating the crime scene?"

"Pretty much. Some kids stole the crime scene tape," he said with a chuckle. "We replaced it to keep people out of there."

"They stole the crime scene tape?"

He nodded. "They do it occasionally. Bragging rights, I guess."

I shook my head. "I just hope you get this figured out soon."

"We will," he promised.

I knew the police would get to the bottom of Amy's murder. And as I thought about it, I became angry. Who would kill somebody as nice as Amy was? That was the question of the day all right, and if I could find out any information that might help Ethan in the investigation, I was going to find it.

Ethan turned and looked at the display case. "I really need to stay away from your mother's fudge, you know."

"Nobody's forcing you to eat it," I teased.

He nodded. "I guess you aren't, but every time I come in here, there it sits. Calling my name, telling me how much I want it. And it's right, I do want it."

We both looked up as the door of the candy shop opened, and Rick Newsom walked in. He smiled when he looked at us. "Hi Mia, hi Ethan. I was passing by, and I suddenly realized that I needed to stop in and get some candy. Well, maybe need is too strong of a word, but I sure do want some."

"Well, you came to the right place," I said, trying not to look at Ethan. Rick was Amy's nurse at the office, and I remembered what Steve Jones had said about him not being able to get along with Amy. "What can I help you with?" I set the owl I had in my hand down on the shelf and headed back over to the front counter to help Rick.

He looked into the display case. "I think I'll get some fudge. I suppose you both heard about Amy Jones?" he asked, turning and looking at me, and then Ethan. "I know you heard about it, Ethan."

"We did. It's a terrible shame," I said. I glanced at Ethan again. I was sure Steve Jones had told him that he suspected Rick Newsom of killing his wife.

"I was going to speak to you and the rest of Amy's staff today. Do you have any idea who might have wanted to kill Amy?" Ethan asked, leaning on the front counter.

Rick looked at him thoughtfully. "I really couldn't imagine who would want to do that. She was nice, and the patients liked her." He shrugged. "It doesn't make sense to me."

"What about her disappearance? Any thoughts on what might have happened there?" Ethan asked.

He shook his head again. "No, I saw her on Friday at work, but I left at 5 o'clock. I had an appointment to get a haircut, so I didn't hang around."

"Was anyone left in the office with her?" I asked.

"Oh sure, there were several people. Mary Diaz, the receptionist, Allison White, the office manager, and probably April Salyers, the gal that does the billing, but I didn't see April. She's in the back office most of the time. We usually work late after all the patients are gone, straightening up and putting paperwork away and catching up on any notes we need to add to patients' files. I would have done the same that night, but I had that appointment, and Amy said it was fine for me to leave."

"I just can't imagine who would do such a thing," I said, shaking my head. "Or what she might have been doing in that vacant house."

"Well, I'll tell you something. Most patients liked Amy, but not all of them. Some patients weren't fans of hers." He looked intently at Ethan and then me.

"What do you mean?" Ethan asked.

He shrugged. "Sometimes Amy got it in her head that she was right about a diagnosis, and she resented it when someone disagreed with her. She could get short with people sometimes."

"Anyone in particular?" Ethan asked.

"Maybe Milton Stinger. But don't tell anyone I said so. They argued in the office when she refused to refer him to a specialist about a certain medical issue he had. HIPAA laws prohibit me from going into detail, you understand."

Ethan considered this. "Do you think he was a threat to her?"

He shrugged. "Maybe not. But when I heard she had disappeared, the thought did cross my mind that he might have gotten even with her."

"Even with her?" Ethan asked. "Do you think he had it out for her?"

He shrugged again. "Maybe. Sometimes people are all bluster. But this guy gets mad at the drop of a hat. He said he'd take care of her one day, and he didn't mean it nicely."

"Isn't he in his sixties and uses a walker? I have to wonder if he would've been capable of forcing her into that house," I pointed out. Steve Jones had said Rick's grandmother had died when Amy wouldn't send her to the hospital. What he was saying about Milton Stinger may have been true, but then he might have his own reason to harm her.

He looked at me. "The walker was temporary. He had hip surgery, but he doesn't use it anymore. And I suppose if he had a weapon, he could've forced her into his car and taken her over there. She probably wouldn't have even fought him if he had a gun. I mean, setting the house on fire was kind of genius, don't you think? Because if he shot her and her body was badly burned, maybe the police couldn't tell that she had been shot or recover a bullet to run tests on."

Rick had a point. If her body was burned badly enough, it would be difficult for the medical examiner to figure out how she died. I looked at Ethan.

He was carefully considering what Rick was saying. "I suppose it doesn't hurt to talk to him."

Rick nodded. "It wouldn't surprise me if a conversation with him turned out to be quite useful to the investigation."

I wasn't sure what Rick was saying was convincing enough for me. He also seemed like he had thought out that scenario pretty thoroughly, and that made me suspicious.

"Rick, is there anyone else that might have had an issue with Amy? Maybe someone that disagreed with a diagnosis she gave?" I asked, hoping he would say something about his grandmother dying.

"Yeah, I'm sure there were a lot of misdiagnoses going on. Doctors don't know everything," he said. His mouth formed a hard line, and he turned back to the candy counter. "This fudge sure looks good. I can smell it through the display case."

I glanced at Ethan and opened the back of the display case. "What kind would you like?"

Rick bought a quarter of a pound of chocolate fudge with nuts and a bag of jellybeans. When he paid for them and left the shop, I turned to Ethan.

"What do you think?"

"I think he thought the situation through pretty well, and that makes me wonder about him. He's right in that the body was badly burned. The medical examiner said it was going to be difficult to get much useful information from it. I'm just glad he was able to decipher through her dental records that it was Amy."

"I guess teeth are pretty resistant to fire?" I said.

He nodded. "Teeth are the hardest substance in the human body. Thank goodness for teeth."

"What do you think about Rick? Do you think there's a possibility he may have had something to do with her death?"

"I'd like to speak with him in private and see what else he has to say. I will definitely be paying him a visit in the next few days."

"It's funny he didn't mention his grandmother dying because Amy didn't send her to the hospital."

"Seems like he would have mentioned that."

"Can you haul him in and interrogate him? Bust some kneecaps?" I asked.

He chuckled and stepped over to the display case. "Sometime soon, I will talk to him. But right now, no, I cannot bust any kneecaps. Maybe later. I also have other people to talk to, and we'll see how things go."

"You're really going to bust his kneecaps, though? I was kidding."

He shrugged. "A cop has gotta do what a cop has gotta do."

I didn't feel good about Rick. He had so readily volunteered the idea that if her body was too badly burned, the police wouldn't know exactly how Amy had died. Either he was putting a lot of thought into this, or he knew what happened to her because he was the one that had killed her.

Chapter Eight

I WASN'T SURE WHAT to make of Amy Jones being found dead in an empty house that was set on fire. She had to have been forced into that house, otherwise, why would she be there? She didn't need a rental that I knew of, although it did cross my mind that perhaps she was. If, as Fagan Branigan had told Christy, she and her husband were having difficulties, maybe she was thinking about separating from her husband. But would she have gone to look at the house late on a Friday night? And if so, where was the owner of the house? While our neighborhood was nice, it wasn't one of the nicest in Pumpkin Hollow. I would have thought she would have bought a new house if she were leaving her husband and he was staying in the house they shared.

I headed to the drugstore to pick up a prescription for my mother. She occasionally had arthritis flareups, and she had called in an old prescription to be refilled. I had insisted she see another doctor about being tired all the time, but she hadn't done it yet.

The long line at the pharmacy counter was disappointing, and I decided to wander the aisles in hopes it would go down if I waited it out. I needed to pick up some moisturizer and mascara, anyway.

I went back to the cosmetics department and looked over the mascaras.

"Hello, Mia," I heard a voice say from behind me. I turned around to look.

"Hi Linda," I said. Linda Reid was a friend of my mother's and a frequent customer at the candy store. "How are you today?"

She chuckled and put one hand on my shoulder. "I tell you, Mia," she said. "This getting old is for the birds. I think I go through a quart of moisturizer every two weeks anymore. My skin has gotten so dry. But I guess it beats the alternative." She laughed again. "How are you doing?"

I chuckled. Linda Reid was one of those people that was always upbeat, no matter the circumstances. "I need some moisturizer myself," I said. "And I'm doing fine."

"Your mother told me you were doing a lot of business with Internet sales these days," she said. "That's good to hear. Businesses that are doing well help a lot of people—both customers and the employees."

"We've certainly been doing a lot more business. Christmas was kind of crazy for us, and we hired some part-time temporary help for Valentine's Day. We're thinking we need some permanent help with all the extra Internet orders."

"Really?" she said, thinking about this. "You wouldn't mind hiring old folk, would you?"

"You aren't old folk, if you're asking for yourself," I said. "Are you looking for a job?"

She nodded. "I've been thinking for months now that I'd like to take on a part-time job. I don't have enough things to do with my time, and my husband says I'm getting on his nerves." She laughed. "I told him if you really want me to get on your nerves, I certainly could arrange it."

"You should talk to my mom about it," I said. "As long as you can pack candy orders and wait on customers, you're qualified." I didn't know how my mom would feel about working with one of her friends. She had known Linda since they were little girls, and I thought Linda would be fun to work with.

"I'm going to do just that. Say, Mia," she said thoughtfully. "I heard about that poor Dr. Jones dying in that burning house. Has Ethan figured out anything about what happened to her?"

"It's too early in the investigation to know for sure, but I'm sure he'll get it sorted out."

She nodded. "You know, I heard she disappeared Friday night, but that's odd because I swear that I saw her Saturday morning."

"Really? Where did you see her?" Amy's husband said she never came home from work, and if it was true that she was seen Saturday morning, then I wondered where she had been.

She thought about it a moment, putting a finger to her chin. "Oh Mia, I am so forgetful some days. But if I remember right, I saw her coming out of the gift shop."

"The gift shop? Ethan needs to talk to Polly Givens then. If Amy was there Saturday morning, it might help him with the investigation."

She nodded. "I think that would be important information to have. If she didn't disappear Friday night as I had heard, that makes you wonder why someone is saying that."

It made me wonder the same thing. "I appreciate the information, Linda. I'll tell Ethan you saw her." I picked up some mascara from the display on the wall. "Don't forget to stop in and ask my mom about the job. It would be fun having you work with us."

"Thanks, Mia," she said, brightening. "I certainly will."

"I've got to get going now. I'll talk to you later."

"All right, see you later, Mia," she said.

I went to check out, forgetting about the prescription I needed to pick up. I decided to have a conversation with Polly Givens to see if she remembered seeing Amy Saturday morning.

THE GIFT SHOP WAS EMPTY of customers when I got there. Polly was at the back of the store with a box of merchandise on a cart and a piece of paper in her hand.

I headed over to her. "Hi Polly," I said. "How are you today?"

She looked up from the paper she was looking over. "Mia," she said, smiling. "I'm doing well. We just got a new shipment of candles in, and I'm going over the packing list to make sure we got everything. I got lots of new scents and sizes in."

I peered into the box to see what she was working on. There were lots of pastels as well as cream-colored candles. I picked up a pale yellow candle and inhaled the scent of honeysuckle. "This smells so good," I said, and then picked up a blue one and smelled it. "Blueberry pie. I could eat this one."

She chuckled. "We get the best candles. I probably have a hundred of them at home. My husband complains, but I can't resist them."

I nodded. "I'd have the same problem if I worked here. Polly, can I ask you a question? Did Dr. Amy Jones stop in here on Saturday morning?"

She looked at me, thinking. Her glasses were on a gold chain around her neck and they had slipped to the end of her nose. "Last Saturday?"

I nodded. "In the morning."

She ran her tongue along her bottom lip as she thought it over. "You know what, Mia? I didn't work Saturday morning. I was trying to remember, but I haven't seen Amy for several weeks."

I was disappointed. "Really? Okay." Linda hadn't seemed too sure, so maybe it was someplace else she had seen her if it had even been Saturday morning.

"Why do you ask? Is it true she was found dead at that house that burned down on Pumpkin Lane?"

I nodded. "I'm afraid so. Someone told me they saw her coming out of the gift shop Saturday morning, and I just wondered if it was true."

She turned around and called, "Carl!"

In a few moments, her husband poked his head out of the back room. "Yeah?" He had a pair of glasses on a chain around his neck as well, and paperwork in his hand.

"Carl, did Dr. Amy Jones come into the shop Saturday morning?"

He thought about it a moment and shook his head. "No, I don't remember seeing her. But, I suppose I could've missed her. I've been working on orders and quarterly taxes back here. Why?"

"Mia was asking about her," she said.

"I just wondered is all," I said to Carl.

"I heard she died," Carl said, stepping out of the backroom. "Seems a shame. I wonder what she was doing at that house?"

"I'm wondering the same thing," I said with a sigh. I had hoped that if she had stopped by on Saturday morning that it would give us a clue as to what happened to her.

"I heard she was thinking about moving her practice to South Lake Tahoe," Carl said. "It's a real shame what happened to her. I always liked her, and she was so young." He shook his head and made a clucking sound.

I looked at him. "Really? I haven't heard she was thinking about moving her practice."

He nodded. "I was surprised about it. I hated to see such a good doctor leave us. When you live in a small town, you don't have a lot of choices for doctors, and she was a very good doctor."

"Who said she was moving her practice?" I asked and sniffed a cantaloupe scented candle. The smell made my mouth water.

He thought about it a minute. "I don't remember. I think one of our customers came in a few weeks ago and told me that."

Her husband hadn't mentioned her moving the practice, and now I wondered if she really had been planning on leaving him. Maybe she planned on renting the house until she could get her office established in Tahoe and find a house there. "I appreciate the information," I said and smelled the cantaloupe candle again. "This smells so good. I've got a ton of candles at home though, so I better not buy another one."

"I told you we get the best candles in," Polly said with a chuckle.

"I've got to get going now. I have to pick up a prescription for my mother at the drugstore," I said, remembering what I had come downtown for.

"Well, come back when you have time and take a look at all the other new items we got in," Polly said. "You might change your mind about needing another candle."

I laughed. "I probably will change my mind on the candle," I said and headed to the door, feeling disappointed. I had hoped Linda really had seen Amy Saturday morning. The information about her moving her medical practice was interesting, though. I needed to let Ethan know about it, and maybe he could find out from Steve Jones if it was true. It seemed like he would have mentioned it when we talked.

"I'll ask our part-time help if they saw her in here, and I'll let you know," Polly promised.

"I appreciate that," I said over my shoulder. "See you both later."

Chapter Nine

THE FOLLOWING DAY I stopped off at the Sweet Goblin Bakery to pick up some donuts for everyone at the candy store. I know what you're thinking. Isn't my sugar intake high enough just working at the candy store without needing to stop off at the bakery? But I was in the mood for a doughnut, and I couldn't leave everyone else out.

Stella Moretti had been the former owner of the Sweet Goblin Bakery, but she had met her demise in an unsavory manner last fall. I pushed open the door and inhaled the scent of freshly baked doughnuts and cookies. It was 8:30 in the morning, and my stomach grumbled.

I smiled at Angela Karis behind the counter. She wasn't one of my favorite people. I was still suspicious of some things she had done before and after Stella had died. But that wasn't any of my business.

I was the only person in the bakery, and I stepped up to the front counter.

Angela smiled at me. Her gold wire-rimmed glasses had a dot of dough on one lens. "Good morning, Mia," she said, sounding chipper. "What can I get for you?"

"Good morning, Angela," I said, looking over the donuts in the display case. The bakery was decorated for Halloween, with the addition of a few bunnies for the upcoming Easter holiday. There was a life-size mummy against one wall and two large plastic jack-o'-lanterns next to it. Strings of orange and black lights lined the ceiling along the walls, and vintage cardboard Halloween cutouts were placed on the walls strategically. Two brown rabbits poked their heads out from behind a large pumpkin near the front counter. I had to hand it to them. They had done a great job decorating. When Stella was alive, she had refused to participate in the Halloween season, and it had been a point of contention between her and many of the other business owners. I peered into the display case. "Everything looks so good."

"Isn't it wonderful weather outside?" she asked me while I tried to make up my mind about what I wanted. "The sun's been shining the last few days, and it makes me think spring won't be too far away."

"Most of the snow has melted, but it wouldn't surprise me if we got some more before spring officially starts," I said, not taking my eyes from the donuts in the display case. "I think I want a dozen donuts and four coffees."

The coffee the bakery sold wasn't as good as what my friend Amanda sold in her coffee shop, but it was still pretty decent. It was caffeine, and it would do.

"Which donuts would you like?" she asked, unfolding a pink bakery box. The cute Halloween print boxes were saved for the Halloween season.

"How about three maple bars, three sprinkle donuts, three lemon filled, and three of those cute blueberry sprinkle donuts," I said, pointing at the round cake donuts with dark blue frosting and sprinkles. I looked over the rest of the items in the bakery case and felt my mouth salivate. I was hungrier than I realized. There were some daisy-shaped sugar cookies in the case alongside an assortment of Easter egg-shaped ones.

"You got it," she said as she went about putting the donuts into the box. "I heard there was a fire down near where you live." Her eyes went to me, then back to the donuts.

I folded my arms in front of my chest. The room was colder than I had expected, even with the ovens in the back. "Yeah, it was just over on the next block," I said and waited to see if she would ask more about it.

She nodded as she put the maple bars into the box. "Is it true they found Dr. Jones in the burned building?" Her eyes went to mine again.

For a moment I considered whether I should say anything else. But you never know who knows what in a small town. She might have details that could be helpful in the investigation, and as much as I disliked her, I needed to know if she knew something. I nodded. "Unfortunately, they did. I just can't imagine what happened to her and why she was in that house, to begin with."

She nodded sadly. "I really liked Dr. Jones. She was one of the nicest doctors I've ever been to."

"She was a sweet person," I said. "It's a terrible shame. Not only has her family suffered a loss, but it's a loss to the community as well."

She nodded again. "You know, Mia," she said carefully. "Maybe I shouldn't say anything, but maybe Ethan needs to talk to Dr. Jones' nurse. Do you know him? Rick Newsom?"

I nodded "Yes, I know him. He comes by the candy store sometimes, and I think he's lived in Pumpkin Hollow all his life," I said carefully, hoping she knew something useful to the case.

She stopped what she was doing and looked at me. "Okay, this is completely off the record, you understand, but I was at that sports bar in Tahoe a couple of months ago with some friends, and he was there. He had a few too many if you know what I mean, and he said some things that I didn't think too much about at the time, but now that Dr. Jones has been murdered, it makes me wonder."

I waited a moment, and when she didn't continue, it was all I could do to keep from rolling my eyes. She knew I wanted this information, and she was going to tease me with it. "What did he say?" I hated to have to ask, but if she was going to play a game, I was going to play along unless what she had to say was pointless.

She nodded and closed the back of the display case and moved over to the next one and opened it. Before answering, she began putting the sprinkle donuts into the box. "Well, he was complaining about her. He referred to her as his boss, and never used her name, but of course, everyone knows where he works, so it's not like it was a secret who he was talking about.

Anyway, he said he really couldn't stand his boss. He said she had no respect for him, and he thought it was because he was a male nurse."

On this bit of information, I did roll my eyes, but she had her eyes on the donuts and didn't see me. "I don't understand how anybody could think it's odd that a man is an RN in this day and age. Especially Dr. Jones. She had to run into a ton of them when she was training to be a doctor."

She made a clicking noise with her tongue and reached for the blueberry donuts. "I know exactly what you're saying. I feel the same way about it, and at the time, I had to wonder whether Rick was just feeling sorry for himself for some reason. But he did say that his boss didn't appreciate his medical knowledge. He said that was the trouble with doctors, they never listen to their nurses, and it was the nurses who have more contact with the patients, and therefore, know more about what was going on with them."

I could agree with the part about nurses having more contact with their patients than the doctors did. After all, doctors didn't have a lot of time to spend with patients. "I have a hard time believing Dr. Jones was dismissive of anyone. She was always so friendly."

She moved over and began filling the box with the lemon donuts now. "I thought the same thing," she said. "But he just kept going on and on about how full of herself she was, and that her ego was bigger than she was." She chuckled. "It wouldn't take much for her ego to be bigger than she was. I don't think she weighed much over a hundred pounds soaking wet."

Amy didn't stand much over 5 feet tall, and I doubted she was even a hundred pounds. "Did he say anything else?"

She looked at me and nodded. "He sure did. He got so angry thinking she was dismissive of him and what he had to say about patient care, that he said maybe one of these days she'd be taken down a peg or two."

I had to keep from biting my lower lip. "He really said that?"

She nodded and moved to the front counter near the cash register, and began folding the box lid down. "That was exactly what he said. When he said it, I turned and stared at him. He was so angry his face was red. He was there with the woman who does the billing at the doctor's office. I forget what her name is now, but she sat there and just nodded. But when he said that about Dr. Jones being taken down a peg or two, she looked at him like she was surprised. Then she nodded and agreed with him again."

April Salyers was the woman that did the billing at the doctor's office. I was surprised she was with Rick at the bar and even more surprised that she agreed with everything he was saying. It made me wonder even more about Rick. Maybe it wasn't other people that had problems with male nurses. Maybe it was him that had a problem with *being* a male nurse.

"Well, that's certainly interesting," I said, trying to sound casual about it. "I'd hate to think that anyone as close to Amy as Rick was would want to harm her in any way. But I'm sure the police will get this thing sorted out and figure out what happened." I didn't want to give her any encouragement to spread this around town. Rick might hear about it, and if he had killed Amy, he might kill again to stop the rumors.

"I'm so glad Ethan is on the case." She looked up at me with that big smile of hers. I didn't trust it. "Pumpkin Hollow has needed someone as thorough and hardworking as he is to sort out the crime around here."

I made myself smile back at her. "He certainly is dedicated. He'll find the killer."

She nodded. "That's exactly what I thought. Dedicated. That's Ethan, all right. I don't suppose he has anyone in particular in mind as the killer?"

I shook my head. "I think it's too early for him to know anything solid just yet."

She considered this, her eyes narrowing in thought. Then she nodded and turned to me. "Of course, it's early in the investigation yet. I'm sure he'll get it sorted out."

"I know he will."

She looked at me. "I almost forgot. When you buy a dozen donuts, we give you an extra one free. A baker's dozen. Lots of other bakeries don't do that these days." She grinned.

I knew what the grin was for. Stella Moretti had refused to give the extra donut to most people. If she liked you, she might give it to you. But there were certain people she made a point of not giving it to. I put one hand in my front pocket. "How about that Boston cream donut over there?" I pointed to the last Boston cream in the display case.

She nodded. "You got it. I'm so glad you stopped in for a chat, Mia. It seems like it's been ages since I've seen you around. You should stop in more often."

I smiled. "I suppose I should."

There was something about Angela that I couldn't stand. And now I knew exactly what it was. She was disingenuous. She may have pretended to be innocent and helpful in passing on the information she had, but she knew exactly what she was doing. She was gossiping and hoping to get information from me in return so she could spread that around. She probably couldn't wait for me to stop in to give me this tidbit of information. I didn't care though. If it would help Ethan solve the case, then it didn't matter how it came to me.

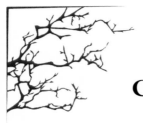

Chapter Ten

I WALKED INTO THE CANDY store and called out, "donuts!"

Christy turned and grinned at me. "Donuts? My gosh, I haven't had a donut in what seems like forever." Then she frowned at me. "Wait a minute, are you trying to keep me from losing those ten pounds?"

I rolled my eyes at her. "What are you talking about? I brought us donuts. Eat a donut and make me happy." I headed over to the front counter and put the box down.

Mom came out of the kitchen. "Did I hear you say donuts?"

I nodded. "And coffee," I said, setting the drink carrier down next to the donuts. "I brought packets of creamer and sugar so you can fix it up the way you like it."

"My stars," Mom said, heading over to the counter and picking up a cup of coffee. "I don't need the donuts, but you know I'm going to have one anyway. And I sure could use the coffee as a pick me up."

I nodded. "It's like I can read your mind. Is Carrie here yet?"

"She'll be in any minute now," Mom said as she took the lid off of her coffee.

The door opened, and I turned as Ethan walked through it. He grinned, his eyes going to the box of donuts on the counter. "Looks like I stopped by at just the right time."

"I wish I'd known you were stopping by, I'd have gotten you a coffee," I said as he came over and gave me a quick kiss.

His eyes didn't leave the box of donuts. "That's okay, I've got one in my car."

"I hope those donuts aren't more interesting to you than I am."

"Of course not," he said, still not looking at me.

I rolled my eyes. "Sure." I went around to the other side of the counter. "I was just in the mood for donuts today and thought I'd treat everyone." I handed him a napkin and opened the box.

"Well, we certainly appreciate it," Mom said. "I think I've made more fudge this morning than I have since Christmas, and I needed a little break."

"Lots of orders?" I asked her and reached for a lemon filled donut.

She nodded. "Lots of orders."

"We are the candy-making queens around here," Christy said and looked over the donuts in the box. "How's the investigation going, Ethan?"

"It's going all right, I guess," he said, picking up a maple bar.

Mom took her donut and coffee back to the kitchen, and after much hesitation, Christy decided on one of the sprinkle donuts. "At least it's smaller than the others," she said, picking up her cup of coffee. "I'll drink my coffee black and save some calories." She went back to join Mom in the kitchen.

I shook my head and turned to Ethan. "Want some of my coffee?"

"No, that's okay," he said and took a bite of his donut. "I love these donuts."

"So Ethan," I said when we were alone. "Anything new?"

"Not a lot. I'm still talking to people," he said, and we both turned to the door when the bell above it jingled.

I smiled when Milton Stinger walked through the door. Mr. Stinger had a weakness for chocolate fudge without walnuts, and before his wife died, we saw him just about every other week. He hadn't been in the candy store since his wife had died. I had taken him some fudge twice since then in the hopes of luring him out of his house. I worried he would become a recluse without his wife around to help him socialize. Mr. Stinger was an introvert.

"Good morning, Mr. Stinger," I said. "How are you today?" I moved the donut box to a shelf below the front counter.

He shook his head. "I'll tell you, Mia," he said. "Things just haven't been the same since Louise died. That, and I've been feeling a little under the weather."

"I'm sorry to hear you haven't been feeling well," I said. "I know you miss Louise. We miss seeing her come into the store."

He nodded. "She loved those chocolate oranges you carry, and of course, the fudge."

"I know, she used to get a chocolate orange at least once a month."

He stopped and looked up at Ethan in his uniform. "How are you, Officer Ethan Banks?"

Ethan smiled, trying to hide the donut in his hand behind his back. "Oh, I'm fine, Mr. Stinger. I'm sorry to hear you aren't feeling well."

He nodded. "I had to switch doctors a few months back. I had to quit that quack, Dr. Jones. I told her she needed to refer me to a specialist for my angina, but she wouldn't hear of it." He sighed and looked confused for a moment. "I suppose I should have quit her a long time ago."

"I hope you'll get along better with your new doctor," I said, glancing at Ethan. Mr. Stinger liked things his way, and Amy refusing to refer him to a specialist hadn't gone over well.

He looked up at me sharply. "I think someone got tired of that quack not referring patients out to specialists."

I glanced at Ethan again. "What do you mean, Mr. Stinger?"

"Someone killed that quack of a doctor the other night, from what I hear," he said, nodding. "I wouldn't blame anyone for doing it. Not that I would kill anyone, you understand. I don't believe in going to that extent. But, when somebody is as incompetent as that so-called doctor was, you can see where someone would get angry and maybe do something terrible."

"What do you mean, Mr. Stinger?" Ethan asked him. "Are you saying you think one of her patients killed her?"

"I don't suppose I know that for certain," he said thoughtfully. "Only that I could see where someone would want to do her in. Look, when you take someone's life into your hands, you should know what you're doing. And if you don't, then go wash windows or something."

Ethan considered him carefully. "It's best not to consider things like murder," he said. "Sometimes, if you think hard enough on something, you end up acting on your thoughts and doing something you'll regret."

He nodded again. "Sure. Like I said, I wouldn't do something like that. I guess I'll take a quarter-pound of that chocolate fudge without walnuts," he said to me. Then he turned back to Ethan. "If I had to guess as to who might have done it, besides another patient I mean, I would guess it was that gal that works in her office."

I went to the back of the display case and removed the fudge he had asked for. "Which one is that?" I asked.

"That girl that does all the billing," he said, trying to recall her name. "April something or other. I told her the doctor wouldn't refer me to a specialist, and I ended up at the hospital emergency room one night because of her, and she agreed with me. She said it was wrong for her not to refer me out, and not only that, the doctor had her bill the insurance company for tests that she never ran. She was trying to cover for herself, you know. Make it look like she had ordered tests that she never ran on me."

"April told you this?" Ethan asked him.

He nodded. "She sure did. She was mad that doctor didn't treat patients right. April told me I should sue, and I've been trying to get a lawyer that will take the case. The trouble is, I don't have any paperwork to back up what she told me."

"I imagine without the paperwork to back up what you're saying, it would have been hard to sue her," I said as I cut the fudge for Mr. Stinger.

"April said she would get me the proof, but she never has. I need to stop by the office and see if she can get it for me now that the doctor isn't around anymore. Seems like no one in that office liked her if you want to know the truth," he said, nodding. "I can see why."

I was surprised he thought no one in the office liked Dr. Jones. Everyone I had spoken to seemed to like her, and I wondered if he was just angry over her not referring him to a specialist.

"I'm sure they're not allowed to give out that kind of information," Ethan said to him, but looked at me. I wondered if the court would order them to hand over the paperwork if it became necessary.

"I tell you," he said, turning to Ethan. "You should talk to April. As much as I appreciate her telling me the truth about what that doctor did, she should've been loyal to her employer, or she should've found another job. She told me that one day someone would pay that doctor back for the things she had done. Makes me think she had something to do with the doctor being killed, but I can't say I know that for certain."

I had gone to school with April, and I thought I knew her well enough to ask her about what was going on in Dr. Jones' office before she died. I decided to visit her and see if she would tell me something that might help with the investigation.

"Sometimes people say things without thinking," Ethan said in defense of April. I knew he didn't want rumors started around town. There were enough rumors already flying because Amy died in that vacant house.

He nodded. "Sure, sure. I guess people do, but that April, she said she'd get me anything I wanted so I could bring a lawsuit against that doctor. She said she was tired of seeing some of the things that went on in that office, and she wasn't going to put up with it anymore. She wouldn't go into any details about what she'd seen, though. I don't know why she hasn't gotten me the paperwork like she promised."

"Maybe she wasn't happy with her job, and she was just blowing off steam," I suggested.

He looked at me. "Still, I'd hate to have someone like that on my staff. She could make a mess of a lot of situations, and I tell you, she was mad about something."

I was definitely going to talk to April Salyers. If she knew anything that could help with the case, I wanted to know about it. And if she had something to do with actually killing Dr. Jones, I wanted to know that, too.

Chapter Eleven

APRIL BAKER WAS A FITNESS fanatic. I knew that much about her. I hadn't been around her much since we graduated from high school, but we would talk for a few minutes when I went in to see Dr. Jones. Sometimes I would run into her at the grocery store or the drugstore, and we always stopped a moment to chat. I'd seen her posts on social media, and I knew she was proud of the body she was building down at the gym.

When I got off work, Christy and I drove to the gym in the hopes she would be there. As I drove into the parking lot, I spied a red SUV, and she had been driving one last summer when I ran into her at the grocery store. It had personalized plates that said WRK OUT, and I was pretty sure it was hers. I pulled into the parking space next to it.

"I need a gym membership," Christy groused. "I've got to get this weight off."

I chuckled. I hoped Ethan appreciated the sacrifice I was making. When I was in school, I had avoided PE whenever possible, and since graduating high school, I avoided exercise unless I had no other choice.

"This place is really big," Christy said, looking up at the building. "I don't know why I've never been in here."

"Probably because you're about as fitness challenged as I am," I explained to her.

She laughed and shook her head.

We walked through the gym doors, and at the front counter, a peppy looking blond woman sat with a water bottle in one hand. She smiled at us. "Good afternoon! Welcome! How may I help you, ladies?"

I smiled, suddenly unsure. All we wanted to do was see if we could find April and talk to her for a few minutes, but now we were faced with what looked like a peppy cheerleader that guarded the way into the weight room.

"We're not members here," I said. "But we wondered if we could just take a look around and see if it's the right gym for us." It was a lie, of course. I had no intention of joining a gym.

She sprang to her feet. "Of course! Let me give you ladies a tour. We'll start in the weight room and move on to cardio. Don't you ladies just love cardio?"

Drats. My eyes went wide as I glanced at Christy, who was looking the place over. I turned back to the woman. "Do you mind if we just have a look around? We'd like to take our time and check things out, and we don't want to take up your valuable time."

"Nonsense! It's no trouble. I'll give you the tour right now," she said, coming around the side of the counter. "You'll love it here. We've got personal trainers and exercise classes going on all the time."

"Do you have lots of treadmills?" Christy asked, peering into the weight room.

"Of course we do. Let me take you around, and I'll show you," she said.

"Why don't we just look around ourselves?" I suggested. "We don't want to waste your time. I'm sure you've got a lot of things you need to do."

She hesitated. "Well, that's okay, I can give you the tour really quickly, and then you can take a look around on your own if there's something you want to get more familiar with."

The smile I had pasted on my face began to droop. What if April was just getting ready to end her workout? What if the length of time it took for Miss Peppy to give us the tour meant I would miss April?

"I tell you what," I said, trying to sound as excited as she was. "Let us take a look, and then we'll come back with any questions we might have. And if we've missed anything, you can show us around."

Doubt flickered in her eyes. "Well, I suppose there's nothing in the rules against you doing that." As she was trying to come up with a reason why we couldn't, her phone rang. "Hold on a moment." She reached across the counter and picked up the phone, and we took that opportunity to walk into the weight room without her. "Hold on, ladies!"

We kept walking without looking back. I didn't have time to be given a tour of a gym that I had no intention of joining.

"We should have taken the tour. I might want to join," Christy whispered.

"I don't want a tour. I'm not joining a gym."

I spotted April in a back corner on a weight machine. She was sitting on the contraption, trying to move a huge stack of weights with her legs. I thought it must be what they called a leg press because she was putting an awful lot of energy into pressing that thing.

"She's over here," I said to Christy.

We sauntered over to April. Her attention was on the exercise she was doing, and she didn't realize we had suddenly appeared at her side. "Hi April," I said, sounding as if I had just spotted her. "What a coincidence. I didn't know you came to this gym."

She glanced up, losing her concentration, and the stack of weights slammed against the machine. She smiled. "Hi Mia, hi Christy," she said, breathing out hard. "Yes, I've been coming to this gym for years now. Are you two joining? I don't remember seeing either of you around here."

I nodded. "We've been talking about it for a while now. With it being spring, we thought, what better time than to start working out now? Summer will be here before we know it, and we want to be in shape when it gets here."

"And we're going to be in Amanda Krigbaum's wedding in June, so we want to lose a few pounds," Christy added.

Her eyes lit up. "That's great! Working out is one of my favorite things to do. And now that I've got a little extra free time, I think I'm going to spend more time down here. I've always wanted to compete in a bodybuilding contest."

I couldn't imagine why anybody would want to do something like that, but I didn't say it. "Really? I know you've always enjoyed working out, but competing in something like that sounds like—fun."

She nodded, excitement showing in her eyes. "I can hardly wait. I've been working on my nutrition and coming up with a plan to get me there by summer."

"So, you have more free time?" I asked.

She nodded. "Didn't you hear about Dr. Jones?"

"Oh, of course," I said. "What was I thinking? Christy and I said what a terrible shame it was when we heard about what happened. I just can't imagine who would do something like that to Dr. Jones."

She shook her head sadly. "I was so shocked when I heard about it. Like you, I don't know who would have done something like that to her."

This was getting me nowhere. "Well, whoever killed her must have had a real grudge against her. I just don't understand people who kill."

She nodded. "Exactly. There are a million and one ways to handle differences or disagreements, and I can't imagine what must go through someone's mind when they decide to kill."

"Did she give you any indication that she might be having trouble with anyone?" Christy asked.

She thought about this for a minute. "Well, I'll tell you," she said, glancing around. "There was this one guy that really scared her a few months back. He started as a patient, but she had the office manager send him a letter to tell him he was no longer welcome as a patient at the office."

"Really? What did he do to deserve that?" I stepped in closer to her.

"Apparently he was stalking her. She said she would look in her review mirror when she was driving, and he would be behind her, or sometimes if she was at the grocery store, he would just happen to be there too, and he always wanted to talk to her."

"Did she say who it was?" I asked.

"Sure, it was Mike Hoffman. I don't know if you know him or not. He's probably in his mid-forties, and before she had the office manager send the letter, he would come in once a week complaining about a sore throat, or allergies, or a rash or something or other. We thought he was a hypochondriac at first, but then Dr. Jones said he was following her around town."

"That's scary," I said, taking this in. I had dated Mike's brother years ago, and I felt like I knew Mike, but maybe I didn't. "So she felt threatened by him? Did she think he would take it further than just following her around town?"

She shrugged. "She didn't tell me that, but she may have said something to one of the other girls. Honestly, it didn't surprise me that she ended up dead."

I stared at her. "Why do you say that?"

"Because of the way she treated people. There was a real lack of ethics in that office, and if a patient dared to question the treatment she was providing, she would get angry and tell them they were lucky she was even taking the time to see them. There were more than a handful of people that she had the office manager send a letter to, telling them they were no longer welcome at her practice."

"I had no idea," I said slowly. "I mean, they just questioned her treatment or diagnosis, and that was it? That was enough to make her decide she didn't want to treat them anymore?"

She nodded. "And another thing—you know I do the billing down there. Sometimes she would lie about the treatment she gave patients. She would have me over-bill insurance companies, and when I questioned her, she became irate. It didn't take long for me to realize I better not question her anymore."

"That sounds like a nightmare," Christy said. "Seems like you'd worry about whether you'd have a job at all."

She nodded. "You better believe it. I didn't want to see her die or anything, but it's kind of a relief not to have to go back there. I was already looking for another job."

"Wow, I guess you don't really know what goes on with some people," I said. What she was saying didn't make sense to me. I felt like I knew Amy well enough to know her character, and the person April was describing wasn't the Amy I knew.

"Exactly," she said, nodding. She swung her legs around on the machine to face us. "That's exactly it. I'm also glad to be getting away from Rick Newsom, the nurse down there. He was a piece of work. He was just as crazy about anyone questioning his so-called medical wisdom as Dr. Jones was. The egos in that office were out of control, and I'm not sorry I won't be going back."

I stared at her. "I don't blame you," I said slowly. "Do you think that Mike Hoffman was capable of killing her?"

She sighed. "I think anyone that goes to the trouble of making up excuses to come in to see the doctor and then follows her around town is capable of just about anything. I mean, come on, that's the kind of behavior you see in people who aren't all there."

I couldn't argue with that logic. A person who stalked another had to either know it was wrong or be completely oblivious to what they were doing. And if he was completely oblivious to it, maybe he didn't intend to kill her. On the other hand, maybe he knew it was wrong and didn't care, and when she wouldn't respond the way he wanted her to, he killed her.

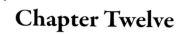

Chapter Twelve

ETHAN WAS TRUE TO HIS word, and when the weekend arrived, he took me to a nice restaurant in Truckee. Truckee wasn't a large town, but they had a nice restaurant that served American food. We were looking over the menu, and I looked up at him. "I've been starving for a good steak."

"Starving? That sounds pretty serious," he said. "I'm glad I got you here when I did. I'd hate for you to faint from hunger."

I chuckled. "It is serious. They have a great porterhouse steak with baked potato and a choice of sides. I had it a long time ago, and I don't know what they put in the seasoning, but it sure was good. I might have to order two dinners. I'm that hungry."

He grinned. "I think I'm going to go with the ribeye steak with béarnaise. It looks good," he said. "But then, there's a bacon mushroom burger that looks good, too."

I nodded, looking at the picture of the burger in question. It was huge and as hungry as I was, I didn't know if I could even eat all of it. "Everything is good here." I laid my menu on the side of the table and looked around the restaurant. It was Friday night, and the place was packed.

The restaurant had once been a seafood place, and along the wall, there was a ship's wheel and some large seashells. On the solid wood paneling, there were cattle brands burned into it near a lasso. It'd been years since the seafood restaurant had closed, but the owners had left the ship's wheel and seashells and offered a few seafood dishes along with the steaks and burgers.

Ethan laid his menu on top of mine and took a sip of his iced tea. "So tell me, what's new with you? Besides making tons of candy every day. Is the candy store world-famous yet?"

I shrugged. "That's my life, you know," I said and took a sip of my iced tea. "Candy maker's daughter I was born, and candy maker's daughter I shall die. As far as being world-famous, not yet. But we're working on it. We're talking about printing up a catalog to send out to our growing mailing list. I guess physical catalogs are considered old-fashioned, but there are a lot of people who still shop that way, and I think it's good to have one available."

He chuckled. "I think a catalog is a great idea. I also think it's a great idea that you're a candy maker's daughter. Lucky for me, that means I get candy, too."

"You've got a great deal there," I told him.

"Don't I know it. I'll have to keep you happy so I can eat free fudge."

I had already told him what April said about Mike Hoffman, Dr. Jones' billing practices, and her nurse. "Are you going to talk to Mike Hoffman? He owns a gardening service in town."

He nodded. "I've seen the truck and trailer he drives around with gardening equipment on it. If that's the same Mike

Hoffman we're talking about, anyway. I'll stop by and talk to him tomorrow."

"That's the one. I don't know that I believe he would stalk Amy. That creeps me out. Somebody that would do something like that has to be unhinged."

He chuckled. "That's what I'm going to put in my report after I speak to him. The subject is completely unhinged."

"I just can't believe it's true."

"We'll find out of it is or not," he assured me.

I sat back in my seat. The noise of the other diners was loud. There was a party going on in the back of the room, and laughter rang throughout the restaurant.

"I also have to wonder about Rick Newsom. A couple of people have mentioned that his ego was out of control. If he felt slighted by Dr. Jones when she didn't pay any attention to his medical expertise, or what he thought was expertise, he may have become angry and killed her."

"That's a good possibility," he said, his gaze on the other diners. "I don't understand people that are so full of themselves. It makes working with them miserable. Maybe he got offended at her and killed her."

"Did the medical examiner get his full report back to you yet?"

He turned back to me. "He did, but there wasn't a lot he had to say. Her body was too badly burned to get much out of it."

I looked at him, surprised. "Was the fire burning for that long before we woke up?"

"The fire department noted an accelerant was used. Apparently, whatever was used was poured directly onto her body, and the fire came close to consuming it."

"Poor Amy," I said, feeling nauseous now. "I prefer to think of her as the nice sweet person I knew her to be, and not the person some people are trying to say she was. Honestly, sometimes I think people are just bitter and angry and have their own agenda when they say those kinds of things."

He took a sip of his iced tea. "It's a possibility. Sometimes people become bitter and jaded about something or someone and project their own issues onto that person. It becomes all about them."

"Do you think Milton Stinger is capable of killing her? He's got to be in his late sixties, and although he's anything but ancient and feeble, I still have a hard time thinking he'd be able to force her to do anything she didn't want to do."

"Unless he had a gun and forced her to go with him," Ethan said. "He seems very angry, but he apparently can't come up with anything in writing saying that Dr. Jones was billing insurance fraudulently."

"I wonder if there's any connection to why Amy was taken to that particular house? There are other empty houses around town. Have you spoken with the owner?"

He grinned at me. "Aren't you becoming a good detective? I've been trying to locate the owner and haven't been able to contact him just yet."

I sat back against the booth's back. "I'm just thinking about all the angles."

The waitress came and took our orders and then left.

"There is one thing I found out," he said, lowering his voice. "The carpet in Dr. Jones' office was replaced the day after she disappeared."

I looked at him. "Wait, she disappeared Friday night and then the carpet in her office was replaced Saturday?"

He nodded. "First thing in the morning. There was a company that came in and pulled out the old carpeting and laid new."

"Who requested that to be done?" I asked.

"Rick Newsom."

I stared at him, taking this in. "Why would Rick Newsom be in charge of having the carpeting replaced in the office? He's a nurse."

"That's a good question," he said. "I'm going to ask him about it tomorrow. I just found out about it late this afternoon. We're going to get a warrant to have the carpet pulled up and see what's underneath it."

"Wow," I said. "She may have been killed in the office Friday night and taken to that house and set on fire. If someone shot or stabbed her in the office, and then remove that carpet to get rid of blood stains, it boggles my mind. Who would be so horrible and devious to do that?"

He nodded. "I called her husband, and he claims he knew nothing about it."

"Rick Newsom has some explaining to do," I said.

"That he does," he said. "I'm also going to go and talk to the manager of the store where the carpet came from. See if he has anything to say about it that I don't already know. Maybe somebody slipped up and said something. Or maybe whoever ordered it, we're assuming it was Rick, seemed overly nervous."

"Wait, how do you know the carpet was replaced if you haven't spoken to either Rick or the company that sold and installed it?" I asked him.

"I spoke to Allison White, the office manager. She said she was surprised to see it because she wasn't aware it was going to be done until she came in on Monday when it was already installed."

"You might want to ask her about sending a letter to Mike Hoffman about not being allowed to remain a patient at Dr. Jones' office. I wonder what the conversation between her and Dr. Jones was like," I said.

"Duly noted," he said. "I've got several people to speak to tomorrow. We'll get to the bottom of this murder."

I knew he would. Someone somewhere was going to slip up, either in the way they had tried to cover up the crime or with something that someone else knew about the killer or the victim. Somehow things would come together, and we would figure out who killed Dr. Amy Jones.

Chapter Thirteen

I HAD A DAY OFF FROM the candy store and as I lay in bed, trying to get a few more minutes of sleep, I heard equipment startup outside. I pulled my pillow over my head and groaned. Opening one eye, I looked at my phone. It was three minutes after eight. I groaned again, and after trying for ten more minutes to go back to sleep, I gave up. I sat up, and Boo jumped on my bed.

"Did they wake you up, too?" I asked and reached out and rubbed his head. Boo responded by purring and leaning into my hand.

I sat on the edge of the bed, swinging my legs over the side. The sun was shining, and it brightened my mood despite having been rudely woken up. I slid my feet into my slippers and headed over to the window, pulling back the curtain. There was a tree near the sidewalk in front of my house that had begun leaning a bit, and the owners of my little cottage must have called someone to cut it down. I wished they had chosen a time later in the day to take care of it. I let the curtain fall back, and I headed to the kitchen to make some coffee.

Boo followed after me, meowing loudly.

"I know, you're hungry," I mumbled and went to the cat food bin and scooped some food out for him, putting it into his bowl. "There you go. That should make you happy." Boo went after the food hungrily, and I chuckled.

I open the cupboard and took down the coffee beans, and put some into the grinder. The equipment outside was even louder in the kitchen, and I managed to drown it out for a couple of minutes when I turned on the coffee bean grinder. With the coffee started, I went back to my bedroom and got dressed. I looked through the window at the men working on the tree again. That was when I realized one of the men was Mike Hoffman, Amy Jones' stalker. Or maybe I should say alleged stalker since we didn't know for sure if he had done it.

I quickly put my boots on, brushed my hair, and headed out my front door. The men didn't hear me come out of my house over the din of the chainsaw, so I walked out into the yard and tried to get Mike's attention. He turned to look at me and smiled when he recognized me.

"Good morning Mia," he said, nodding. He stepped away from the guy who held the chainsaw so we could talk. One of the good things about small towns is that everybody likes to stop and visit. "I hope we didn't wake you up."

"I needed to get up, anyway. I've got all kinds of laundry and errands to run today. How have you been, Mike?" Mike had done yard work for my parents in the past, and I'd run into him around town from time to time.

He nodded. "Pretty good. With spring beginning, we're getting a lot more calls. The next six weeks or so, I expect we'll be working longer hours with all the additional work."

I nodded. "That tree has been slowly listing to the side since last fall. I mentioned it to the owners, and they said they'd check it out, but I never heard anything back from them."

He nodded. "They asked me to stop by last week and take a look at it, and honestly, I'd hate for it to fall on someone. I recommended they take it out as soon as possible."

The guy holding the chainsaw was Mike's oldest son, and when he noticed me, he smiled. "Hello!" he called.

I nodded. "Hi Jake," I called back.

"I'm glad you're taking the tree down," I said. "I don't know much about trees, but it worried me a bit."

"No problem. We'll get it down in no time and get it hauled off," he said.

"How has Timmy been?" I asked. Timmy was a nice guy, but I had gone off to college, and he stayed behind in Pumpkin Hollow. We'd both gone on to date other people that lived closer to us.

"He's doing okay. He got married a couple of years ago, and he's working in construction now. How have you been?"

I shrugged. "I moved back to Pumpkin Hollow last summer, and I'm dating Ethan Banks these days."

"Ethan Banks? He's a police officer, isn't he?"

"He is. He got a promotion recently, and he handles the more serious crimes that require investigation, like murder, when they need him to." I waited to see if he would bring up Amy Jones' death.

He whistled. "Really? Well, good for him. I bet he's excited about doing that kind of work." He said. Jake continued working on the tree, and we took a couple more steps away from him to get away from the sound of the chainsaw.

"He really is," I said. "He enjoys the puzzle of looking at clues and finding the culprit. I think he gets a lot of satisfaction from putting people behind bars that have committed terrible crimes." I waited. Would he mention Amy? Or was I going to have to find a way to bring it up?

He thought about it a moment. "Didn't Dr. Jones die recently? Seems someone mentioned that."

I nodded, glad he had brought it up. "Yes, it was a terrible shame. Her body was found over at that burned house," I said, pointing at the house on the corner. There was still crime scene tape around the outside.

He turned and looked at it, narrowing his eyes. "That really is a terrible shame. Does Ethan know who the killer is yet?"

"Not yet. These things just take time to sort out, but I know he's going to find whoever is responsible for her death."

He turned back to me, his face solemn. "I hate to hear about that kind of thing. She was a good doctor, and I know she did this community a lot of good. I can't imagine who would do such a thing."

"I can't either," I said, agreeing. "I really liked Amy."

He nodded. "I used to go to her a couple of years ago," he said carefully. "She was a good doctor. But you know, if I were Ethan, I might stop in and talk to that nurse of hers."

When he didn't continue, I said, "Her nurse? You mean Rick Newsom?"

He hesitated before answering. "Yes, him. There was something not quite right about him."

I folded my arms against the cold morning air. "What do you mean? Not quite right?"

"He just seemed to have a chip on his shoulder. Last spring, I had an allergic reaction to some crab salad I ate. I didn't have an appointment, but I stopped in to see if she had time to see me. She was busy, and he said if it were him, he'd consider going to a doctor that knew what they were talking about."

"He said that to one of her patients?" I asked.

He nodded. "He did. I was shocked he said something like that, and I asked him what he meant. He just rolled his eyes and said never mind. She can handle it."

That was an odd thing for a nurse to tell a patient, but it backed up the other stories I'd heard about Rick's and Amy's working relationship. "Did he ever say anything else?"

He nodded. "He told me another time that her license was almost suspended once for misdiagnosis of a patient."

"Wow." I couldn't understand why a nurse would say that about the doctor he worked for. "That's incredibly unprofessional behavior. I would think Amy would have wanted to feel she could trust the people that worked for her and that they supported her."

"Wouldn't you, though?" He shook his head and chuckled disdainfully. "Some people don't know the meaning of loyalty. I'll tell you something else. Because of Rick Newsom, Dr. Jones sent me a letter saying she didn't want me to be a patient anymore." His jaw tightened, and he wouldn't meet my eyes.

"What do you mean? Why would she do that?"

He shrugged. "When I called him on not being loyal to his employer, he got mad. He was clenching his teeth and said it was none of my business. I told him he needed to be loyal to the doctor he worked for and that he shouldn't try to drive off her patients."

"What was the reason given in the letter?"

He looked at me, his eyes flashing with anger. "It said I was behaving inappropriately. She said I had been following her around town." He snorted. "Following her around town? I have a business to run! I don't have time for that kind of thing, and I don't have any reason to do something like that. She didn't come out and say it in the letter, but it sounded like she thought I had some sort of romantic interest in her. I love my wife. I can't imagine thinking about another woman that way."

I looked at him wide-eyed. "Why do you think Rick was behind her sending that letter?"

"Because I saw him after I got the letter. We were at the grocery store, and he just turned around and stared at me, and then he gave me this smile that said, 'I took care of you'. I almost went over there and punched him in the face, but I didn't want to get into any trouble." His hands clenched into fists as he spoke, and his face turned red.

"What an awful thing for him to do," I said. I wasn't sure if I believed Mike or not. If he was innocent, I could see why the incident made him angry. But there was something about his reaction that made me wonder.

"You can say that again," he said. Then he breathed out and seemed to relax.

"But if Amy said you were following her around town, she had to have seen you," I said carefully. I didn't want to make him any angrier than he already was.

He chuckled bitterly. "Sure, I happened to be driving behind her a couple of times on my way to job sites. I remember seeing her personalized license plate. It was a coincidence. But I can imagine Rick lying to her about me, and her just happening to see my truck behind her a couple of times. She probably jumped to conclusions based on what he told her."

It was a possibility. But I still wasn't sure I believed it. "I guess that could happen."

He nodded. "It's the only explanation I can come up with. Believe me, I've racked my brain over it all. Well, Mia, I guess I shouldn't be digging up stuff that should be left in the past. It doesn't do anyone any good, does it?"

"No, it sure doesn't. But I do understand why you would be so angry about what he did."

He nodded again. "I better get back to work," he said. "It's good seeing you again."

"Tell Timmy I said hello when you see him," I said and headed back into the house.

If what he said was true, then Rick had even more explaining to do.

Chapter Fourteen

I HADN'T PLANNED ON doing much of anything on my day off. Ethan was at work, so there wasn't a lot for me to do. Christy was working and Amanda was at the coffee shop. I took another sip of my coffee and sighed. There was always laundry and dishes to wash, and if the truth be told, I hadn't dusted or vacuumed the house since before Valentine's Day. I wasn't even sure how I'd gotten behind on the housework, but I suspected it had something to do with the increased business at the candy store. The Internet sales were a boon to business, and by the time I got home in the evenings, I didn't want to do anything.

I drained my coffee cup and went about collecting the dirty cups in the living room, and took them to the sink. There were several plates, silverware, and two more cups in it. I rinse them quickly and put them into the dishwasher, added soap, and turned it on. There. That had taken about three minutes of my time.

Next, I took my dirty clothes hamper to the tiny laundry room at the back of the house. It really wasn't a room, it was more of an alcove that the washer and dryer sat in. When I first moved in, I had borrowed Ethan's washer and dryer, and even with as close as he was, it was still easier to have my own washer and dryer in my house. I got the laundry started and headed to the living room to start dusting. Boo rubbed up against my legs in an attempt to dissuade me from doing the housework. He would have been happy for me to sit on the couch all day so he could sit in my lap and be petted.

"I can't stay here and pet you all day," I told him. I bent over and rubbed his head and then got to work.

When I had finished with the housework, I looked out the front window to see how the tree removal was going. The tree was down, and they had already cut it into pieces and were now putting the pieces of the tree into the back of their truck. I wasn't sure what to think about what Mike had told me. He hadn't tried to hide the fact that there was a letter requesting him not to come back to Amy's practice, and that made me think he was telling the truth about what Rick had said to get that letter written. But there was something about his anger over the situation that bothered me, and I wondered if there was something he wasn't telling me.

It didn't make sense to me that as a nurse, Rick thought he knew more than the doctor he worked for. At the very least, he shouldn't have been so open about it. Discretion seemed to be lacking in that office. I sat down on the sofa and opened my laptop to catch up with my friends. I wasn't sure if social media was a blessing or a curse. While it helped me stay caught up with friends and family who lived far away, it prevented me from picking up the phone and talking to them. It was just easier to send them a private message.

It wasn't long before I heard Mike's truck pulling away, and I set my laptop down on the coffee table and went to the window. There was a cut off stump nearly level with the ground where the tree used to be, and I wondered if they would come back later to remove it or if it would stay.

My eyes went to the burned house where Amy's body had been found. I wondered if the owner had come in to take stock of the damage yet. I grabbed my keys and locked the door behind me, and took a stroll over to the house. Standing in front of it, I looked up. There were burn marks on the outside near one of the windows that was now covered with plywood. I looked around the neighborhood to see if anyone was nearby, but the neighborhood appeared empty.

There was a six-foot-tall solid wood fence around the backyard of the house. I headed over to the gate. It opened easily, and I walked around to the back door and gave the doorknob a turn. I found it was locked. Next, I checked a side door that led to the basement, and that one was unlocked. The firemen may have forgotten to lock it behind themselves the night of the fire.

I headed into the darkened basement and stopped. I didn't know if they had shut off the electricity, but I tried the light switch and found it wouldn't turn the lights on. I pulled my phone out of my pocket and turned the flashlight on, pointing it at the floor in hopes that it wouldn't alert anyone. With it being daylight outside, I didn't think anyone would see it, but I wanted to make sure. I headed up the stairs and into the house.

Ethan had said Amy's body had been in the living room, so I headed there. The house was empty, and it was cold inside. I got to the end of the hallway and stopped. There was a large, burned-out area on the living room floor. I swallowed and tried not to picture Amy lying there.

Carefully, I walked closer to the burned-out place on the floor. Burn marks were going up the wall and to the ceiling in that area. I turn the flashlight to the area on the floor. There was debris there, probably from when the firemen had turned the hose on the fire. Part of the ceiling had fallen nearby, and there were pieces of drywall on the floor.

I walked carefully around the area, trying to find anything that might be of interest. The police had already been in here, as well as the fire department, and I doubted there was anything left behind, but I looked anyway. I put the toe of my boot against the debris on the floor and scooted it aside. It was still heavy and wet with water. Insulation from the ceiling had fallen into the pile, and I moved it around some more with my boot. I wondered if there was asbestos in it and decided I wouldn't touch it with my bare hands.

A car drove by, and there was a flash as the sun hit the windshield, and I jumped. When the car was safely down the street, I turned back to the pile of rubbish. I could see dark black wavy marks on the floor and on the nearby wall, and I wondered if that was left from the accelerant that was used. I began kicking around in the debris but found only pieces of drywall and insulation.

After a bit, I gave that up and walked through the rest of the house. It was empty and fairly clean, considering what it had been through. Had the house only been a convenient place to try to dispose of Amy's body? Or was there another reason she was brought here?

I headed up the stairs, hoping I wasn't getting myself into trouble. I put both hands on the stair rails, and when I got to the top, I turned to look down at the burned spot and shuddered. It was a horrible way to die, and I hoped she was already dead before she was set on fire.

I looked through the three bedrooms and two bathrooms that were upstairs, and it was as clean as the unburned areas of the downstairs. I headed back downstairs and to the back door, unlocked it from the inside, and left that way, locking the door behind me again. I didn't want to get caught in this place, but I stopped to take a look at the area around the house itself. There were rose bushes in the front of the house and in the back, and there were small shrubs and larger bushes, but there wasn't much of anything to be seen that looked suspicious. There were some empty places where it looked like shrubs had been removed. The snow had completely melted, and the owners probably had yard work done when the last renters had moved out because the yard was neat and clean. The ground was marked by a rake that had been used back here, but a tall pine tree leaned against the back fence, looking brown and dead. Why hadn't it been removed with the shrubs?

The clouds in the sky moved across the sun, and when they had passed, the light shined down, and I saw something beneath a bush. I bent down and picked it up.

Staring at it, I turned it over. It was a silver charm in the shape of a medical symbol and had the letters R and N.

Chapter Fifteen

I PICKED UP THE CHARM and looked it over, then I slipped it into my pocket and bent over, moving the branches of the shrubbery to see if anything else was there. Laying near where I picked up the charm, there was a broken silver chain. It looked expensive and heavy, like something I thought a man might wear. I picked it up and slipped it into my pocket along with the charm. I spent another twenty minutes carefully going over the ground around the doors and windows of the house in the backyard, but I didn't find anything else.

I heard a vehicle pull up and stop, and I thought it must be parked at the curb in front of the house. I hurried to the gate and slipped through it, glancing toward the front of the house. A work truck had parked along the curb, the kind that did home repairs or light construction work. I headed to the sidewalk on the side of the house and acted as if I had been walking up the street. I stopped at the corner and looked in the direction of the house. The driver had his head down, and I continued across the street and back to my house.

Once inside, I grabbed my purse and keys and headed back outside, locking the door behind me. I needed to find Ethan and show him what I had found. Once inside my car, I called him, but he didn't answer his cell phone. I slipped the phone into my purse and backed out of the driveway.

ETHAN WAS IN HIS OFFICE at the police station. I headed back, after saying hello to the officer at the front desk. Pumpkin Hollow was small enough that they didn't mind me stopping in to see him once in a while. If I brought candy, I was sure they wouldn't mind if it was an everyday visit. I hadn't stopped to pick any candy up, but I didn't get so much as a sideways look from the other officers as I went back.

Ethan's door was open, and I knocked on it, then stepped inside. He looked up at me and smiled, his blond hair shining beneath the fluorescent lights.

"Hey, there's my pretty girlfriend," he teased.

I sighed. My heart was still pounding in my chest from what I had just done. I shouldn't have been inside that house. Ethan wouldn't give me too much trouble over it, and I was sure the necklace in my pocket was the answer to the mystery of who killed Amy Jones. The thought made me almost giddy. Putting killers behind bars was beginning to excite me.

"Hey," I said and went to him. Leaning over his desk, I kissed him. "Guess what?"

One eyebrow lifted. "What?"

I pulled the silver chain and charm from my pocket and laid them on his desk. "This."

"What is that?" he asked, eyeing them.

"I stopped by the burned house, and these were in the shrubs near the back door. The chain looks like it was broken. Maybe Amy struggled with the killer and pulled it off."

He picked up the charm, looking at it carefully. "It's a nurse's charm."

"Yes. And we know her nurse had issues with her."

"Excuse me," a voice said from behind me.

Ethan and I turned to see who it was. Steve Jones walked into the office, his eyes drawn to the charm in Ethan's hand.

"What are you doing with Rick Newsom's necklace?" he asked. He came to stand beside me in front of the desk.

"How do you know it's Rick Newsom's necklace?" Ethan asked him.

"Amy gave it to him when he got his RN license. It was a gift. She wanted to give him something to commemorate the achievement."

Ethan looked at me, surprise showing in his eyes.

"How do you know it's the same one Amy gave him?" I asked, turning to him. It was a simple charm, one you could probably find almost anywhere.

He shrugged. "She had his initials engraved on the back. RSN. It's very tiny."

Ethan turned it over. On the back, in very tiny letters, was RSN. I hadn't noticed it when I picked it up. My breath caught in my chest.

Ethan looked up at him. "Did Amy know Rick before he became an RN?"

"Sure. He worked for her as an LPN before he got his RN license. A Licensed practical nurse. She encouraged him to get his RN license. He wasn't sure he wanted to do it, but Amy told him an RN would earn more money and there was no reason for him not to. She even gave him time to study during the day when it was slow." He looked from me to Ethan.

Ethan nodded slowly. "Would there be a reason it would be at the house where Amy's body was found?" he asked him.

Steve's eyes got big. "It was at the house where Amy's body was found? I told you he killed Amy!" His face turned red, and his hands curled into fists.

"Steve, calm down. We are still investigating your wife's murder. We need to look into this, and I'd appreciate it if you wouldn't talk to anyone about it," Ethan said calmly.

"There might be a plausible reason it was there at that house," I said. I knew there wasn't, but I hoped it would help calm him down. What other reason could there be? Rick Newsom had killed Amy. He had more reason than anyone else did to kill her. I took a deep breath.

Steve suddenly went pale, and he inhaled deeply. "This makes me sick. I can't believe it. I mean, sure, I thought he might have done it, but I know this means he really did do it."

I pulled a chair from the corner of the tiny room and moved it over to the front of the desk. "Have a seat, Steve," I said, then I pulled another one from the other corner and sat down. Ethan's office was tiny, and he pushed his visitor's chairs to the corners to make more room in front of his desk.

Steve sat down heavily. "Amy helped him get into nursing school. She spoke to the dean of students and wrote a glowing letter of recommendation. She had such hopes for him and really encouraged him."

I was surprised to hear this after all I'd heard about Rick and Amy's rocky working relationship. "I thought they didn't get along?"

He turned to me. "They didn't. After Rick graduated, he changed. He said he hadn't needed Amy's help and told everyone that he got into the school on his own merits. It wasn't true. He only got average scores when he tested. If it weren't for Amy, he would never have gotten in. The animosity between the two of them grew as the years went on."

"When did Rick graduate from nursing school?" Ethan asked him.

"It's only been about six or seven years, but it was a rough six or seven years, let me tell you. His attitude upset Amy something terrible. She regretted ever having helped him."

Ethan glanced at me. "Is there anything else you can tell me that might help in the investigation?" he asked him.

He sighed wearily. "There is something else that you probably should know." He kept his eyes on a spot in the middle of Ethan's desk and was quiet for a minute. "He tried to get Amy to have an affair with him. She refused. She wasn't like that. It's part of the reason for the animosity."

I was surprised at this news. "What do you mean, tried?"

"He kept telling her he loved her and that she should leave me. She wasn't interested in him, and she told him that. I guess it must have hurt his pride. He kept trying to get her to go out with him, and finally, Amy had to tell him to drop it, or she would have to let him go. She said he wouldn't speak to her for weeks afterward."

"Why would Amy put up with that?" I asked. I couldn't imagine having to work with that sort of thing hanging in the air. If it were me, I would have fired him.

"She felt sorry for him. He was going to marry Alissa Dean, and she died of cancer three months before the wedding. He was devastated, as you can imagine, and began to drink some. Amy thought helping him get into nursing school would help him get his life on track again. She had a soft heart for people that had had a tragedy in their lives."

I nodded. "I can see that. She was always so caring," I said. But I wondered about the other rumors. "Steve, how was your marriage?"

He looked at me a moment before answering. "I guess you've heard the rumors? Our marriage was fine. Sure, we'd had a few recent bumps, but who doesn't? We were going to go on vacation this summer for a couple of weeks. Hawaii. We just wanted to spend some time focusing on each other. The only reason there are rumors is because of Rick. Amy and I were both told by different people that he was talking about us." He snorted. "The only real trouble we had was him."

"Is it true that she was thinking about moving her practice to South Lake Tahoe?" I asked.

He nodded. "She was thinking about it. We looked at homes there, but we hadn't made a decision yet."

Ethan sat back in his chair, taking this all in. His eyes went to the chain and charm on the desk. He picked up the chain and examined the ends of it. It had been broken. Torn off Rick's neck. I shuddered. Poor Amy.

Ethan looked at Steve. "I've got to take this to the chief and discuss what we know. I need you to keep this quiet. Not a word to anyone, not even your family."

Steve nodded. "Just arrest my wife's killer. That's all I ask. Arrest her killer and send him away forever."

"We'll do our best," Ethan said.

I sighed. In a situation like this, the best that could be done was to arrest the killer and let the judicial system do its job. It wouldn't bring the victim back, but it would at least give the victim's family closure.

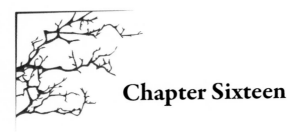

Chapter Sixteen

ETHAN WALKED THROUGH the door to the candy store looking tired. Peeking through the blinds at his house across the street, waiting for him to come home, the previous night had worn me out, and I finally went to bed at midnight without getting a chance to catch up with him on what was going on. I would have liked to have called and checked on him, but I hated to bother him when I knew he was working on something so critical. Arresting a killer must be stressful, I thought.

He smiled tiredly at me.

"What time did you get home?" I asked him.

He sighed and leaned on the front counter. "About 2:00 a.m."

"Wow. What took so long?"

"Interrogation. Oh, excuse me. Interview." He grinned. "I have to remember the correct terminology."

I chuckled. "As long as you didn't bust any kneecaps."

He shook his head. "No busted kneecaps."

"So, he's in jail?" I hated to ask him too much at this point. It was early yet, and I always felt like I was being nosy when I asked too many questions.

"He's in jail." He glanced around the shop, but we were alone. Mom and Christy were in the kitchen. "He denies everything."

"Of course. I wouldn't admit I had killed someone. He has nothing to lose by lying."

"True. He denied everything Steve told us, of course. He kept trying to tell us about the problems Amy and Steve had in their marriage."

"Of course. Deflect the guilt. It makes me so angry. How could he have killed her like that? He's in the health care profession. He should value human life." I wasn't stupid enough to think that all doctors and nurses were saints, but it bothered me that someone could take a life so easily.

"You know what the interesting thing was?" he asked.

"What?"

"He said he hadn't seen that necklace for more than a year. He claims he lost it."

"What?" I repeated. "Lost it? Do you believe him?"

He shrugged and yawned. "That will be up to a jury whether they believe he's telling the truth or lying. He had the motive, and he had the means. Oh yeah, and that carpet he had replaced in the office? He claims Amy told him to have it replaced because it was old, but there's nothing to prove it." He went over to the display case and looked in. "That peanut butter fudge sure looks good."

"It is good, as always," I said, thinking these things over. "Did they pull up the carpet in the office?"

"Sure did. We sprayed luminol, but nothing showed up. I was hoping there'd be something there. It would help get a conviction."

"Why would Amy ask her nurse to order new carpet? Wouldn't she have asked the office manager to handle that?" I asked him. "And if she was contemplating moving the practice, why spend the money to update the office here?"

"You would think the office manager would handle that. Doesn't make sense that she would spend the money on new carpet if she was possibly moving, does it?"

I sighed and went and opened the back of the display case. "Peanut butter fudge?"

"I thought you'd never ask."

I chuckled and pulled out the tray. "I know you can't resist the fudge. Neither can I."

"MIA, I'D LIKE TO DROWN my sorrows in candy," Steve Jones said when he walked through the door.

I smiled at him. "Well, you came to the right place. What can I get for you?"

"Let me take a look," he said and went to look into the display case. "It all looks so good. Your mother is a genius when it comes to candy."

"I know she is. I'm a little jealous that she's so talented." I leaned on the front counter while he made his decision.

"Nonsense. I bet you're just as talented," he said. "That praline fudge looks good."

"It's wonderful," I said. Steve looked like he'd had a rough night. His shirt was unbuttoned at the top and was wrinkled. His graying hair was uncombed, and one sleeve was rolled up while the other was down.

"I suppose you know that Rick Newsom was arrested," he said without looking at me.

"I did hear that," I said. "I guess you can breathe a sigh of relief now."

He looked at me. "No, not really. Amy is still gone. As much as I had hoped finding her killer would set my mind at ease, I was wrong. I don't think things will ever be okay for me again." He sighed sadly.

"I'm sorry. That was thoughtless of me to say. I can understand that things will never be the same for you."

He nodded. "It's hard for a person to understand what one goes through when the love of your life is murdered. I had no idea. But I guess, now I know." He turned back to the display case. "Why don't you give me a quarter pound of the praline fudge and a quarter pound of the fudge with walnuts. At least I can drown my sorrows in sugar."

"I'll get that for you," I said and went to the display case and removed the trays.

"Did Ethan say what happens next?" he asked as I cut and weighed the fudge.

"Not really. I think it's out of his hands now. The case will go to trial, of course, but his job is done until he has to testify, I think."

He nodded. "I just can't thank him enough for what he's done. At least there's closure now. Amy's parents came out for the funeral, and they were so distraught, as you can imagine. It will help them to rest easier now."

"At least there's that. I wish things could have turned out differently," I said sympathetically. I couldn't imagine having to live with the fact that a loved one had been murdered. It was unthinkable.

"I never did find out how that necklace was found. Did Ethan happen to mention that?" he asked.

I wrapped the peanut butter fudge in waxed paper and slipped it into a white paper bag. "Oh, I found it at the house where her body was found." As soon as I said it, I thought it was the wrong thing to say. I didn't want anyone to know I had been snooping around.

"You found it?" he asked, surprised.

I looked at him guiltily. "I guess I was snooping. It made me feel so bad that Amy had been murdered," I said weakly.

He nodded. "Well, I appreciate it. Who knows how long it might have been until the killer was caught if you hadn't found that necklace?"

I smiled and began wrapping the praline fudge. "I need to keep it to myself, I guess. It isn't my business, and I shouldn't snoop."

"Oh no, you won't find me complaining about it. You did me a great favor. I appreciate it."

I smiled and rang his order up. "I just wish this had never happened. She will be greatly missed."

He ran his debit card through the card reader. "You can say that again. Life will never be the same again."

I handed him the bag of fudge. He took it from me and hesitated, not looking at me. "Tell me, Mia, does Ethan think it will stick? The murder conviction? I'd hate for the evidence of that necklace to be dismissed because you found it and not the police."

I felt my face go pale. "We haven't discussed that."

He looked at me now. "It would have been better if the police found it. A jury wouldn't question it if the police found it. I don't know why they didn't come across it when they searched the premises."

I swallowed. I should have left the necklace where it lay and let Ethan find it. "I don't know about those kinds of things, I guess."

He nodded. "Of course not. Who would have thought of something like that? You tell Ethan to give me a call when he can, will you?"

"Of course," I said. My mouth had gone dry, and my stomach heaved at the thought. Had I made a terrible mistake? Had I made it impossible to convict Rick of murder by picking up that necklace?

"Well, I had better get going then," he said but made no move to leave. He looked at me as if waiting for me to say something more.

I nodded. "Sure, I'll see you, then. Ethan will give you a call."

"All right, you have a good evening," he said, and this time, he turned and left the store.

I watched him go, feeling sick. I needed to call Ethan. Had I made a mess of things? I suddenly felt like I had.

Chapter Seventeen

"HELLO, MIA," MIKE HOFFMAN said. He came and stood near me as I unpacked a box of pastel-colored saltwater taffy to fill the bulk bin with.

I looked up at him and smiled. "Hello, Mike. How are you this afternoon?" We had had a few quiet days in the wake of Rick Newsom's arrest, and things were finally getting back to normal, or what felt like normal, here in Pumpkin Hollow. Amy Jones would be sorely missed; a hole that was left in the town.

He grinned sheepishly. "I'm doing all right, I guess. Ever since I spoke to you the other day, I've had fudge on my mind though. I'm not supposed to eat it, on account of high cholesterol, but I'm going to have to get some, anyway. It's all I can think about, it seems."

I chuckled and stood up. "My mother's fudge does that to a person. You'd think that with working here, I'd get burned out on it, but I still have to have some from time to time. What kind can I get you?" I headed behind the counter, stowing the now empty packing box the taffy had come in back in the corner.

He stepped up to the display case and peered in. "What kind is that?" he asked, pointing at one of the trays.

"That is penuche. The recipe comes from Italy, and its fudge made with brown sugar and butter. It kind of tastes like a cross between butterscotch and vanilla. It's really good."

His eyes lit up. "That sounds good. What's that one?" he asked, pointing at another tray.

"That is mint chocolate chip fudge. That's also really good if you like mint and chocolate." Mike wore a red and black flannel shirt, jeans, and black work boots. A white t-shirt poked out where the top button was undone on the flannel shirt. I was glad Mike hadn't killed Amy. I liked Mike, despite the rumors that he had stalked her. At this point, I knew it was nothing more than rumors.

"I do like mint and chocolate. And now, what is that one?" he asked, pointing at another tray. "I'm not good at decision making, as you might have gathered. Sorry for taking up your time."

I chuckled. "It's no trouble. That is orange cream fudge. My mother worked on that one for a while to get the flavor just right. I think she did a great job on it."

"Wow, you're really making my decision hard." He chuckled.

"I understand about indecision. I struggle with it every day when it comes to which candy to choose. I have to limit myself to only one piece per day, or I'll get into trouble with it."

He nodded. "That's a great way to handle it. Unfortunately, I don't think I'm going to have that much self-control. Why don't you get me a quarter pound of each of those three?" he asked. "They all look too good to decide on one."

"You got it," I said and opened the back of the display case. "When in doubt, try them all out."

He laughed. "It's the only way to go. Just don't tell my doctor."

"Your secret is safe with me." I cut a slab off the orange cream fudge and weighed it.

"Say, Mia, speaking of doctors, I heard Rick Newsom was arrested for Amy Jones' murder," he said, sticking one hand into his front jeans pocket.

I glanced at him and nodded. "Yeah, he was arrested the other day. I still can't get over him murdering her. Murder is such an awful crime."

"You can say that again. I knew he was a jerk, and I guess I might have suspected him as the killer, but it's still hard to imagine someone actually stooping to murder. Especially killing someone like Amy."

I glanced at him again as I cut a piece of the penuche. "I'm with you on that. I just don't understand it."

He shrugged. "Well, I guess there's no accounting for some people."

"You and Jake did a good job on that tree in front of my house. I don't have to worry about it falling over now."

He smiled. "Thanks. It's better to take it down before it falls down and hits someone or causes property damage. I was just over at that house where Amy's body was found. There was a dead pine tree that needed to come out. I felt bad being there, just knowing what had happened to her there."

I looked up at him as I cut the mint chocolate fudge. "Really? They had you removing that dead tree already?"

He nodded. "Yeah, I have to wonder if the house is salvageable, but maybe it is. The owner had me pulling out some bushes a couple of weeks ago. I don't know why he didn't have me cut the tree down then."

I looked at him. "When did he have you take out the bushes and shrubs?"

"I guess it was a day or two after the fire. As soon as the police had done their investigation."

That didn't make sense. Why would the owner of the house be so concerned with dead bushes when a body had been found inside and the house set on fire? "Who owns that house?"

"Gerald Cook. When he called, I went down and got the work done right away."

I began wrapping the fudge, thinking this over. "Did Ethan know he hired you to do that?" I knew Gerald, and I couldn't imagine why he would want the yard work done so soon after the fire.

His brow furrowed. "I don't know. I didn't tell him. I didn't think about it. Why?"

I shrugged. "No reason, I guess. It just seems odd."

"Well, to be honest, I thought it was odd, too. But he wanted it done."

"Did you notice anything unusual when you did the work?" I asked, putting the fudge into a paper bag.

"No, I don't remember anything unusual. We took out a couple of rose bushes in the front and cleaned up a little."

"What about the area in the back around the small shrubs? Did you clean up around there?"

"Yeah, one of the bushes back there was dead, and we pulled it out along with some smaller shrubs. Why?"

"And you didn't see anything?" It hadn't taken me long to find the necklace and charm.

He shook his head slowly. "No. Why?"

I stared at him. How could I have found that necklace so quickly if Mike and his son had been back there cleaning up and raking the ground? Wouldn't one of them have seen it? I forced myself to smile and shrugged. "I don't know. I guess I was wondering if there was anything there the police had overlooked."

He smiled now. "It was pretty clean back there. Honestly, other than the dead bushes, all we did was rake up."

I nodded, thinking this over, and rang his purchase up for him. He ran his credit card through the card reader. "Did you ask him why he wanted the yard cleaned up so soon after the fire?"

"I pointed out that he might want to wait until the police said it was all right to do the work. He said he needed to get the work done, and it would be fine. I sure hope we didn't do anything wrong. We were just doing the job we were hired to do."

He looked worried now. I smiled. "Oh, I'm sure it's fine. Especially now that the killer has been arrested. I'm just being nosy." I handed him the bag of fudge.

"Well, you tell Ethan if he needs to talk to me about it, he can give me a call."

"I wouldn't worry about it," I said, waving away the offer. "I hope you enjoy the fudge."

"Thank you. I know I will."

I watched him leave, wondering about what he had told me. If I owned a house that had been set on fire and a body discovered there, the last thing on my mind would be to have some dead bushes removed from the yard.

Chapter Eighteen

THE GROCERY STORE WASN'T one of my favorite places, but it was an unfortunate necessity. If I didn't stop in there at least once in a while, it was a cinch that I'd be eating more fast food than a girl has a right to. And so, I headed to the grocery store after work.

I had already filled the bottom of my grocery cart with produce and whole-grain bread, trying to stick to healthier fare. I'd have to make dinner for Ethan for a week to make sure none of the vegetables turned into science experiments at the back of my refrigerator.

I headed over to the meat department. If I made a roast, I could make good use of the potatoes and carrots I had picked up. Fruit salad might also be in order, or the bananas and apples would go bad.

I looked in at the meat counter. Fortunately for me, pot roasts were on sale, along with chicken breasts. I waited my turn as the woman behind the counter waited on an older man.

"Hi Mia," I heard someone say. I turned to look.

"Oh, hi Gerald. How are you?" I smiled. Gerald Cook was exactly the person I needed to see. What Mike had said earlier had been bothering me. I had called Ethan and told him about it, but he was getting ready to go into a meeting at work and didn't have time to talk to me about it.

"I'm just fine. I'm just stopping in for a few things for my wife. I hate grocery shopping. I never know what to get," he said with a chuckle.

I laughed. "I'm not a fan either, and I do know what to get. The salmon looks good, but it's expensive."

"You can say that again," he said, looking into the display case.

"Gerald, I was so sorry to hear what happened at your rental house. And poor Dr. Jones. It's terrible."

He nodded, looking somber now. "I can hardly believe what happened. I liked Dr. Jones, and I was so sorry to hear someone murdered her. The house was important, but it obviously doesn't compare to a life."

"I couldn't agree more. Are you going to be able to salvage the house?"

"I think so. The insurance adjuster was out yesterday, but I'm still waiting on him to get back to me on it. I certainly hope I'll get enough money to fix it, otherwise I don't know what I'll do. I can't afford to fix it myself. I'm going to retire come June." Gerald had graying hair and looked to be well past retirement age already, and it made me wonder if he just hadn't aged well.

"You are? I bet you can't wait," I said.

"You can say that again. I put in my years at Grenville International Paint and I'm more than ready to go. Not that it was a terrible job, because it wasn't. I'm just ready."

I nodded, leaning on my shopping cart. "I don't blame you. I bet it will be nice to have your time be your own."

He chuckled. "It will be a dream come true. Everyone down at the office is about ready to eat their hearts out, wishing they were me."

"Doesn't Steve Jones work there with you? I feel so bad for him."

He nodded. "Yes, Steve is a manager there. He works in the sales department. It sure has been a shock to everyone there. It's hard to know what to say to a person after their wife has been murdered."

"That's understandable. I don't think there's anything that can be said that will do much to help. It's just a terrible shame. Are you going to rent that house out again?"

"I'm thinking about selling it. I think I'm done with rentals. People are always leaving the place in worse shape than when they first moved in, and it costs me a small fortune to fix it up again when they move out."

"I bet," I said. "Did the last renters leave it in a mess?" I hadn't known the people that lived in the house. They weren't from Pumpkin Hollow, and I had never gotten the chance to meet them.

"Oh, sure. They let the bushes and shrubs die. I just had Mike Hoffman pull the dead ones out. There's a tree in the back that was dead, too, and he removed it." He shook his head.

"Seems like people don't care about things anymore. If it isn't their property, they don't do anything to take care of it."

"That's awful," I said. "When did you have Mike do the work?"

He thought about it. "Oh, I don't remember exactly. Seems like it's been a couple of weeks ago. I only had him do the tree today. I forgot all about it being dead until he reminded me."

"Was it before Amy died, or after?"

"Well, I'd have to look back on my calendar. It might have been right before, but I can't remember right now. It's a real shame about Amy, though. The funny thing is, I don't know how she got in there. I lost the key, you know. I thought I had it in my desk at work, but then when I went to look for it to show the house to a realtor, I couldn't find it."

"Really? The key went missing?" It seemed strange he had lost the key, and then someone ended up dead in the house. It couldn't be a coincidence.

He nodded. "Sure did. But then the house caught fire before I could get a locksmith out there to make me a new key. Honestly, I think I must not have gotten the key back from the renters. My memory isn't what it used to be. My wife is always on me about it."

"Maybe that was it," I said, thoughtfully. Even with a faulty memory, I thought he would have remembered if he hadn't gotten the key back.

He shrugged and chuckled. "I tell you, I can hardly wait for retirement. I'm going to fish to my heart's content. No more getting up at five in the morning unless I want to. But if I'm getting up to go fishing, I have a feeling five o'clock won't be a hardship anymore."

I chuckled. "It's amazing how much easier it is to get up in the morning when you're going to go somewhere you really want to go."

He nodded. "Sure is."

The woman behind the meat counter finished up with her customer, and I stepped forward to tell her what I wanted. I suddenly had a funny feeling that things weren't what they seemed with the case.

Chapter Nineteen

"WHAT WOULD YOU SAY to the idea that maybe Rick Newsom didn't kill Amy Jones?" I asked Ethan over dinner. For all my efforts to buy healthier food while at the grocery store this afternoon, we were now staring down a large pepperoni pizza with mushrooms and jalapenos. What can I say? All that shopping made me tired and hungry, and I didn't feel like cooking.

His brow furrowed. "What do you mean Rick Newsom didn't kill Amy? Why would you say that?"

I looked at him, considering how to tell him what I'd found out. Hadn't Rick Newsom killed Amy? Was I stirring up a hornet's nest by bringing this up? But if an innocent man was in jail, I had an obligation to tell him.

"Mike Hoffman came into the candy store and said he had pulled out some dead shrubs and bushes at the house on the next block."

"The house that Amy's body was found in?" he asked and took a bite of his pizza.

"The one and only."

He chewed and swallowed. "And?"

"And he cleaned the yard two days after her body was found. And he didn't see the necklace that I found."

He stopped chewing, considering what I was saying. "Maybe they overlooked it."

"Maybe. But if he was raking around the bushes and pulling them out, don't you think he would have seen it? It was laying right there in the open. There wasn't anything obstructing it."

He took a drink of his iced tea. "He crossed crime scene tape to do it?"

"He didn't mention it. He said the owner said it was okay to do the work."

He sat back in his chair. "Someone removed it. We thought it was kids fooling around and we put more up."

"Seems odd to me."

He closed his eyes for a minute. When he opened them, he asked, "Who hired him to do the work?"

"He said it was Gerald Cook, the owner of the house. But I saw Gerald at the grocery store, and he couldn't remember what day it was that he called him to do the work. He also said the key to the house turned up missing. He had had it in his desk at work."

"That's odd," he said slowly.

"You can say that again," I said. "And even odder is that Steve Jones just happens to be his co-worker."

He set his slice of pizza on his plate. "Steve Jones. There was a lot of talk about him and Amy arguing."

"And Rick Newsom hadn't seen that necklace in a year."

"How would Steve have gotten ahold of it?" he wondered.

"I don't know, but maybe he saw it lying around and picked it up. Maybe it was there at Amy's office, and he took it."

"And he sure wanted to point a finger at Rick."

I sat back in my chair. "What do you think?"

"I think it's worth having a chat with Steve Jones. I just might pay him a visit soon."

WHILE ETHAN WAS DECIDING what to do about talking to Steve Jones, Christy and I decided to pay him a friendly visit. He was a grieving widower, after all, and we thought he'd appreciate someone checking on him. We brought along some vanilla fudge. It had been Amy's favorite. He might have appreciated the reminder.

"Oh, hello, Christy. Mia," Steve said when he opened the door. The look of surprise was unmistakable. It could have been simply because he wasn't expecting us, but I wondered if it might be something more.

"Hello, Steve," I said, trying to sound happy and perky. I didn't want him to become suspicious of anything. We hoped to get information from him, and if he thought that was the purpose of our visit, he might clam up.

"How are you two today?" he asked, looking at Christy now.

"We're fine. We just thought we'd stop by and check on you," I explained. "We know losing someone is hard, and we wanted to make sure you knew that our hearts are with you during this difficult time." Now I was starting to sound like a Hallmark card.

He nodded slowly. "Well, won't you both come in?"

"Yes, thanks," I said.

We followed him into his house. Cardboard boxes were sitting around the living room, some sealed and others half-full.

"Looks like you're doing a little packing," I said. "Are you going somewhere?"

He turned to look at me. "Yes, I'm moving to Connecticut. I have family there. It's just too painful to stay in this town. I miss Amy too much, and the memories are more than I can handle at this point."

"That's certainly understandable," I said, glancing at Christy. "We brought you some vanilla fudge." I held the bag out to him.

"That's kind of you," he said and took the bag from me.

"I'm sure having to deal with the memories of a lost loved one can be daunting," Christy said. "Especially when that loved one was murdered. It's something no one should have to go through."

He smiled, but it seemed forced. "You have no idea. I think a change of scenery will be good for me. Please, won't you sit down?"

We took a seat on the couch. "Steve, didn't you grow up here in Pumpkin Hollow?" I asked. I didn't know he had family in Connecticut.

He nodded. "Yes, both Amy and I did. But I have cousins in Connecticut, and they invited me to come and stay awhile. I've never lived outside of California before. I think it will be a good change."

"Have you given notice at your job?" Christy asked. "I heard Gerald Cook was retiring. It will be rough for the company to lose both of you at the same time."

He stared at Christy, his eyes getting larger. "I suppose it will take some getting used to for them. They'll have to hire and fill both positions, but they have good management there, and I'm sure they'll find a couple of people to take our places." He looked away, then looked back at us.

"You know, it's a funny thing," Christy said. "But Mia ran into Gerald at the grocery store, and he mentioned he had lost the key to the house where Amy was found. Said he had it in his desk there at work, but it disappeared."

"It's odd that it disappeared like that," I added. I studied his face as we said this. His eyes widened slightly.

"Well, Gerald's memory isn't what it used to be," he said slowly. Pink began to creep up his neck, and he inhaled deeply. "We've been concerned about him for some months now. I think retirement will be good for him."

"It's funny that there was yard work done right after the murder, and the gardener didn't find that necklace that belonged to Rick Newsom. The crime scene tape was mysteriously removed from the property when the yard work was done."

Steve narrowed his eyes at me. "I can't imagine how the gardener didn't see the necklace. Maybe he didn't do a thorough job on the yard. It's hard to find good help these days."

"Or it wasn't there," Christy said. "I wonder why the necklace wasn't there right after the murder? The police didn't find it. The gardener didn't find it. And yet, it suddenly appeared a couple of weeks later."

"It's funny that it appeared after you spread around accusations that Rick and Amy had problems at work and he wanted a relationship with her and was angry she turned him down," I pointed out. Things were progressing quickly. I hadn't planned on making accusations, but one thing had led to another, and here we were. I kept my eyes on Steve, wondering what he would say next.

"I didn't kill my wife," he said through clenched teeth.

"No one said you did," I said amicably. I smiled.

"I think you two need to leave." Steve got to his feet. "You've overstayed your welcome."

We stood up. "You killed Amy, didn't you?" Christy asked quietly.

I glanced at her. I wouldn't have come right out and said it, but I wasn't sorry she had.

He narrowed his eyes at her. "Get out!"

I put a hand on Christy's arm and pulled her toward the front door. "Let's go."

"You killed your wife!" Christy hollered at him as I pulled her away.

"Get out!" he shouted. "Get out of my house!"

We hurried out of the house, and he slammed the door behind us. I turned to look at Christy. "Are you out of your mind?"

"Maybe. But that was kind of fun. We should do this more often."

I groaned, and we hurried to the car, glancing over my shoulder in case Steve changed his mind about letting us leave and came after us. When we'd pulled away from the curb, I called Ethan.

Chapter Twenty

CHRISTY AND I SAT ACROSS from Ethan at Amanda's coffee shop. She was busy behind the counter, waiting on two teenaged girls that appeared to be indecisive.

"So? What gives?" Christy asked him. She took a bite of her blueberry scone, her eyes on him.

Ethan chuckled and took a drink of his coffee. "Steve Jones killed his wife."

When we told Ethan about our visit with Steve Jones, he had stopped by to have his own chat with him. One thing led to another, and Steve had said just enough for Ethan to take him in for questioning. It didn't take long before Ethan got the story out of him.

"Why?" I asked. "They seemed like such a cute couple. I always thought they were happy." It broke my heart that Steve killed Amy. I liked both of them and couldn't imagine how things could have gotten so bad that murder seemed a viable option.

"They were on the verge of getting a divorce. Things were getting ugly. Steve wanted more money to spend as he pleased, and Amy wasn't going to give it to him. Things blew up one night, and he lost his temper and choked her. He claimed it was done in the heat of the moment, but he somehow managed to take out a one million dollar life insurance policy six months earlier."

"Oh. Wow." When he put it like that, I could suddenly picture every ugly detail, and it made me feel sick.

"Oh wow, is right," Christy said, staring at Ethan. "How do you lose your temper suddenly and kill someone? And a one million dollar life insurance policy? Yeah, the heat of the moment, my eye."

"I suspect it was more than once that he lost his temper with her, and things finally escalated, but he won't admit to it. He claims she insisted he buy the insurance policy, just in case, but of course, no one believes that."

I sighed. "Why did he take her to the empty house and set her on fire?" I asked. Part of me didn't want to know, but the part that needed to know the whole story won out.

"He said he panicked when he realized what he had done. He tried to revive her, but it was too late. She had told Steve he needed to move out of their house. He had looked at the house where her body was found, thinking he might rent it for a while. He borrowed the key from Gerald and never gave it back, and Gerald couldn't remember giving it to him. After he killed Amy, he thought he might be able to get rid of her body by setting it on fire."

"Wow," I repeated. "I can't imagine setting someone on fire, let alone someone you love. Or at least used to love."

"He clearly didn't know what he was doing when he brought her there and set her on fire," he said, "because it didn't work."

"I don't buy it," I said, taking a sip of my coffee. "None of it was an accident. He bought the insurance policy and then bided his time, waiting until he thought there had been enough time since he bought it that no one would think anything of it."

"She wouldn't give him money, so he decided to get his own by cashing in on her death. He had the key to that house and took her there in the middle of the night, hoping no one would see the fire for a while and give it some time for her body to burn," Christy said.

"But it wasn't enough time," I added. "I bet he waited a block or two away and watched it burn."

"Probably made him mad the fire department was called so quickly," Christy added.

Ethan chuckled, sitting back in his chair. "The two of you are becoming good little detectives. I don't doubt anything you've both said."

I sighed. "She was so tiny. It wouldn't have taken any effort for him to kill her. What a jerk." I dipped a biscotti into my vanilla latte and took a bite. "I hope he goes away for a long time."

"I hope he at least gets life in prison," Christy said. Then she looked up at me. "That was fun. We should investigate more crimes together."

"It was fun, wasn't it?" I agreed. Christy and I made a good team. I was glad she hadn't stayed away from Pumpkin Hollow. I missed her when she was gone.

"Whoa, wait a minute," Ethan said, holding up one hand. "There will be no more investigating for the two of you. That was more than enough. You're both lucky he didn't hurt either of you. Or both of you."

"I think I'm going to get a gun," Christy said. "That way we'll stay safe."

"No," Ethan warned. "No guns. The two of you are now retired from investigative work."

She rolled her eyes. "You're no fun."

I laughed. "Poor Ethan is going to have a nervous breakdown if we keep investigating."

"That's the truth," he said. "I mean it. No more investigating."

"Fortunately for you, Amanda's wedding is going to be here before we know it, and we've got a lot of work ahead of us to help her pull it off." I eyed him. "We'll be too busy to help you out for a while."

"Good. Help Amanda with the wedding. Stay out of trouble. I've got to get back to work." He stood up, leaned over, and kissed me. "Stay out of trouble. You too, Christy."

"Aye aye, captain," she said and saluted him. He rolled his eyes and headed for the door.

"See you, Amanda," he called over his shoulder.

I turned to Christy. "We better stay out for trouble for a while. Give him a break."

She nodded. "Sure we will."

The End

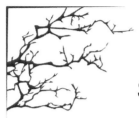

Sneak Peek

C andy Kisses and a Killer
        A Pumpkin Hollow Mystery, book 8
Chapter One

WEDDING PLANS ARE SOMETHING that takes a lot of, well, planning. There are so many details to take care of, so many tiny little things that, if not handled in an appropriate timeframe, will trip the whole thing up. It was June fifth, three days before my best friend Amanda Krigbaum's big day. Under normal circumstances, Amanda was cool as a cucumber, a veritable block of ice under pressure. Now? She was what some might call a little freaked out. Okay, a lot freaked out. A melted block of ice. A puddle of emotions.

"Oh my gosh, Mia, what am I going to do?" she nearly shrieked. Her face was red, and her hair was coming unpinned from the updo we had been practicing for the big day. Handfuls of her blond hair streamed down the side of her face, the humidity causing her almost curly hair to frizz in a most unbecoming way.

I placed both hands on her upper arms and gave her a light shake. "Amanda. It's fine. Everything is fine. Our dresses have been fitted, and they're hanging in our closets. The cake has been ordered, and we've checked on it umpteen times. Invitations were mailed out weeks ago, and we've got a lot of RSVPs back. Our moms are on top of the decorations. This is going to be the most put together, planned out wedding on the face of the planet."

She looked at me warily. "Are you sure?"

I nodded. "I'm positive. Trust me." We were in the kitchen of my parents' candy store, she having just run over from the coffee shop she and her fiancé, Brian Shoate owned, the Little Coffee Shop of Horrors. We celebrated Halloween year-round in Pumpkin Hollow, hence the name of her coffee shop.

"But what about the photographer? I haven't heard from her in weeks."

"I talked to her last week. She is delighted to be able to capture your big day for all of eternity," I assured her.

She inhaled deeply, and then exhaled, allowing her face to come back to a more normal color. Then she smiled and her eyes teared up. "Thank you, Mia. You're the perfect best friend. A girl couldn't ask for anyone more faithful than you."

I smiled back. "Amanda, you're my best friend. There's no way I would allow your wedding day to be a mess. We've all been working so hard on it, and I know it's going to be perfect."

"Oh," she whimpered and started to cry. She pulled me to her and hugged me so tight I thought my eyes would pop out. "I love you, Mia."

"I love you too, Amanda," I croaked. I wanted to push her away so I could get some air, but we were having a moment and moments are important. "Did you sleep with your hair like that?" I hadn't expected her to leave her hair in the updo overnight. The bobby pins must have been uncomfortable.

"Yes. Why?"

I chuckled as she held onto me tightly. "No reason."

After a couple of minutes, she stepped back, her hands still on my shoulders. "What about the caterer? Does she have everything she needs? Is she going to make those cute little pinwheel thingys that everyone likes?"

I nodded. "Christy spoke to Erica four days ago. She went over the menu with her, and Erica assured her everything was ready to go. Pinwheels and all."

"Does she understand that she must be there with everything set up by 6:30? She can't just show up at 6:30 and start setting up. Everything, and I mean everything, has to be on the table and ready for the guests. Oh, maybe I should have told her to be completely set up by six o'clock. What are we going to do now? What if she can't get it all done before the guests are ready to eat?"

"Amanda," I said firmly. "She understands that the guests are going to be arriving around 6:15, and they will be looking for food. There are hors d'oeuvres to start, and then we'll have dinner. There are the candy and ice cream bars, and later there will be cake. Everything is fine."

"Beverages?" she asked.

"Got it. Iced tea, water, coffee, and champagne for the toast. Everything is great. I promise."

Having our moms and my sister Christy and I handling all the details might not have been the smartest move. But in the beginning, it had been exciting, thinking about planning the wedding and making sure everything was taken care of. The tiny little decorative touches seemed like fun. But as the big day drew closer, I think we all wondered if we had made a big mistake. It was all those little details that were throwing a hitch in the thing. We were all worn to a frazzle, running here and there, attending to this and that, and making and attending appointments. In a word, we were exhausted.

She sighed. "You're the best, Mia."

"So are you, Amanda."

"It's so sweet of your mom to give us the candy bar as a wedding present," she said with a sigh. "Really, it was more than I ever could have asked for."

"She thinks so much of you and Brian," I said. "It was one of the first things she thought of when you set the date." Mom was a sucker for weddings. She never put any pressure on me and my boyfriend Ethan, but I knew she was hoping. The truth was, so was I. I just wasn't ready to say anything to Ethan yet. We were enjoying just dating for now. But maybe someday...

"Mia, I think we have trouble with the caterer," my sister Christy said, walking through the door to the kitchen. When she saw Amanda, she stopped, her eyes going wide. "Oh."

"What?" Amanda said, spinning around to face her. "What do you mean, trouble? What kind of trouble?" Her face went pale.

"Oh, um, no, that's not what I meant," Christy said, looking at me for help. "No, see, I just meant that we need to look into something." She pleaded with me with her eyes, but I had no idea what she was talking about.

"What's going on, Christy?" I asked and said a silent prayer that she was being dramatic about something trivial and there wasn't a real problem.

"Tell me what's going on," Amanda demanded. "Tell me everything's okay. Mia, you said everything would be okay." She looked at me sternly. Amanda was my best friend, but her moods had become unstable over the past two weeks, and I didn't blame her for it. A wedding was a lot of pressure.

Christy swallowed. "I can't get ahold of Erica. I wanted to check on the time again, just to be sure, because let's face it, Amanda, you're getting a little hysterical, and I didn't want her to be late."

I rolled my eyes. Calling her hysterical wasn't going to help anything.

"What do you mean, hysterical?" Amanda nearly shrieked. "I'm not hysterical!"

"You're kind of hysterical," Christy said matter-of-factly.

"Christy!" I hissed.

"Okay, I'm sorry, you're not hysterical, Amanda. I shouldn't have said that. I'm sorry. This whole wedding business is becoming stressful for all of us."

"Well, I'm sorry to have made your life stressful," Amanda said tearfully. "I didn't want it to be stressful for you."

Christy went to her and hugged her. "I'm sorry. I would do this for you any day. I didn't mean that. You're going to have a fantastic day. We'll get it sorted out."

Amanda sniffed. "I'm sorry, too," she said. "Maybe we should all go and talk to Erica?"

"Hi girls," Mom said, walking into the kitchen. She carried two empty trays and headed to the sink. "What are you all up to?"

"The caterer isn't answering Christy's phone calls," Amanda said weakly. "I think we need to go talk to her in person."

"Oh? Maybe she's just busy working on the food for the reception," Mom said, turning back to her. "I've got to get a few more things made for the reception, too."

"See? Mom isn't worried about it. But let's go and talk to Erica anyway," I suggested. "Mom, can you spare me for a few minutes?" Christy had worked the earlier shift and was already off the clock, but things had been slow all day, and I knew she wouldn't mind me leaving for a while.

"Of course, Linda will be in any minute now."

"All right, let's go and have a talk with Erica. I'm sure Mom is right. She's probably working on recipes for the reception," I said, trying to sound positive for Amanda.

"I hope so," Amanda said.

So did I. We had all had visions of a fun, carefree wedding, with everything coming together seamlessly. Well, seamless hadn't happened, but there was still no reason to think things wouldn't come together for the big day. We still had about forty-eight hours to take care of all the last-minute details.

Buy Candy Kisses and a Killer on Amazon:
https://www.amazon.com/gp/product/B07VJFSJJJ

If you enjoyed this book, please consider leaving a review. It helps me with visibility on Amazon.

For information on new releases, follow me:
https://www.facebook.com/
Kathleen-Suzette-Kate-Bell-authors-759206390932120/

Manufactured by Amazon.ca
Acheson, AB